Soup's Hoop

BOOKS by ROBERT NEWTON PECK

A Day No Pigs Would Die
Path of Hunters
Millie's Boy
Soup
Fawn
Wild Cat
Soup and Me
Hamilton
Hang for Treason
Rabbits and Redcoats
King of Kazoo (a musical)
Trig
Last Sunday
The King's Iron
Patooie
Soup for President
Eagle Fur
Trig Sees Red
Basket Case
Hub
Mr. Little
Soup's Drum
Trig Goes Ape

Soup on Wheels
Justice Lion
Kirk's Law
Trig or Treat
Banjo
Soup in the Saddle
Fiction Is Folks
The Seminole Seed
Soup's Goat
Dukes
Spanish Hoof
Jo Silver
Soup on Ice
My Vermont
Soup on Fire
Secrets of Successful
*   Fiction*
Hallapoosa
The Horse Hunters
Soup's Uncle
Arly
Soup's Hoop

Soup's Hoop

ROBERT NEWTON PECK

Illustrated by Charles Robinson

Delacorte Press

Published by
Delacorte Press
Bantam Doubleday Dell Publishing Group, Inc.
666 Fifth Avenue
New York, New York 10103

Library of Congress Cataloging in Publication Data

Peck, Robert Newton.
  Soup's hoop / by Robert Newton Peck ; illustrated by Charles Robinson.
    p. cm.
  Summary: Soup's crazy plan to help his town's basketball team to victory includes constructing a musical instrument called a spitzentootle and snaring the evil Janice Riker in an unpleasant trap.
  ISBN 0-385-29808-0
  [1. Basketball—Fiction. 2. Vermont—Fiction. 3. Humorous stories.]
I. Robinson, Charles, ill. II. Title.
PZ7.P339Ssh 1990
[Fic]—dc20   89-34896
                                     CIP
                                      AC

Manufactured in the United States of America

April 1990

10 9 8 7 6 5 4 3 2 1

BVG

Soup's Hoop is dedicated to teachers and parents and friends who read books to children. Especially if the books are written by . . .

Robert Newton Peck

One

"Faster," said Soup.

The two of us whipped our trot to a gallop, rolling Soup's hoop between us. The hoop was merely a thin circle of wood.

It was the first day of May. Spring had arrived, and the muddy dirt road was drying into a lighter-colored dust. An early morning sun was already up and whistling, promising a shiner of a day. Soup and I were on our way to school to confront the mysteries of mathematics.

Soup's abilities at arithmetic were far superior to mine. As far as my brain was concerned, which wasn't very far, I rarely challenged the postulates of either John Napier or Pythagoras. At least I had finally memorized most of my multiplication table, all the way up to seven times nine is forty-four.

Soup was my best pal.

His real name was Luther Wesley Vinson (as mine was Robert Newton Peck) but nobody called him Luther. Except, for some strange reason, his mother. The neighbors called him other things. Some of the expressions they yelled at him I didn't fully comprehend, such as . . . "Get away from my strawberry patch, you little basket."

We ran along the upper flat stretch of road, heading for town, and then stopped at the very top of Dugan's Hill. From here we could view the entire little Vermont village of Learning. Off to our right, a flock of gray woolly sheep were coming down from the hills, driven by a hardworking sheepdog. Several lambs were there too.

"Rob," said Soup, "let's play a prank on the sheep."

At the word *prank,* my hair stiffened. Soup's mischief, in the past, had usual resulted in plunging the two of us into disaster.

"We'll be late for school," I said.

"No we won't," Soup said. "Besides, it isn't a mean prank. It'll be all in fun, and it's sort of on our way to the schoolhouse."

"Okay," I sighed. "What is it?"

Soup grinned. "We'll just climb over the fence, roll my hoop down the meadow hill, and then see what the sheep do when they see it coming."

I agreed.

Soup's hoop was just a light flat-wood barrel ring, about two feet in diameter, too flimsy to hurt any of the sheep. Besides, some of those playful little lambs might see some sport in it.

"Well," said Soup, "here she goes."

He gave his hoop an enthusiastic launching. Down the meadow hill it rolled, gaining speed, and hopping over the gray rocks that freckle most every Vermont pasture.

"Hey," I said, "it's really taking off."

Faster it rolled, bounding higher with every bounce, as though Soup's hoop was enjoying the freedom of a down-hill ride. As it approached the sheep, they eyed it with interest, then with alarm, and scattered in several directions. Yet only far enough to elude the threat of contact. The hoop kept rolling and then disappeared around the corner of one of the shearing barns.

"Come on, Rob. Better we locate it before some disapproving grown-up grabs it for keepers."

Down the meadow hill we raced, whooping, hurdling the smaller rocks and dodging the larger ones. The placid sheep observed us with little or no interest, the way only sheep can look at simpletons. Rounding a corner of the shearing barn, we stopped, and looked for Soup's hoop. No luck. Somehow the hoop had vanished into the melting mists of a May morning.

"It's gone," Soup was moaning.

"No it isn't. A hoop doesn't scoot off somewhere and

hide. The doggone thing's got to be around here somewhere."

"But where?" Soup asked me, shrugging his skinny
shoulders in a futile gesture of despair.

We looked.

Both of us knew that we couldn't be late for school.
Searching for Soup's hoop would hardly serve as an ade-
quate excuse for tardiness, not to Miss Kelly's sterling
standards of attendance. Any student in her one-room
school (there were twenty-eight of us) who arrived late in
the morning would remain in the afternoon. Five minutes
late amounted to ten minutes longer, an eternity under
Miss Kelly's ticking clock and her stern supervision. Plus a
lecture on the virtue of punctuality.

"I guess it's lost," I said.

Soup scratched his head. "Hard to believe. We both saw
it go rolling around this corner."

As we stood in the shadow of the shearing barn, we
continued our search for Soup's hoop. Yet it wasn't to be
found. Meanwhile, the flock of sheep and lambs kept mill-
ing around, bleating their objection to herding, and the
dog was barking. But I thought I heard another sound. It
was neither sheep nor sheepdog.

This sudden and foreign noise seemed to be coming
from above my head. Looking up, I saw nothing but a
morning sky. My pal, apparently, had heard the same
sound, and Soup Vinson was also looking this way and
that, his face becoming a gradual study of confusion.

Again I heard the ominous sound.

It was a laugh. Not a chuckle of joy, but a dirty snicker, one that represented a potential threat to my safety and physical well-being.

Then I heard a whir.

"Rob," asked Soup, "what was that?"

Glancing upward, I saw a very strange sight, one that made me blink. It was something I'd never seen before. Yet there it was, sailing around and around in a circle above the roof of the barn. Or rather in a half circle, because it would appear, disappear, then reappear.

It was Soup's hoop.

What caused it to fly in circles was the fact that the hoop was now tied to a rope. An old rope. From down on the ground where I stood, I could see that the rope was hardly new. It was old and frayed. Someone, however, was holding the rope, swinging it around and around, like a cowboy's lasso.

Its loop was Soup's hoop.

Too late, I saw who was twirling the lasso, recognizing a face only too familiar to every kid in our town of Learning. Fear stuck in my throat like a large glob of frozen peanut butter. I heard Soup gulpingly speak her name.

"Janice."

It was too bad to be true. But there stood Janice Riker, ten feet above us on the edge of the barn's roof, glaring down at Soup and me with her yellow eyes.

At that precise moment, no one had to tap my shoulder

to remind me that a rope and Janice Riker were a danger-
ous combination, especially if the rope had a loop. I'd
come to despise rope. And a rope with a lasso loop on one
end and Janice on the other struck terror in my soul.

In the past, I'd been bound to a tree by Janice and left to
die. Not any old tree. Her tree was above a skunk's den.
I'd also been hog-tied to a telephone pole upon which
hung a hornets' nest, and also was nearby to a generous
pile of cow manure. Small wonder why, at this very moment of a May morning, all my pores seemed to be hollering one little word.

Help!

"Rob," said Soup, "we gotta run."

We ran.

At the same split second, Soup Vinson bolted in one
direction, and I darted in the other. Trouble is, we were
still looking up at Janice, and we ran smack into each
other, just as the lasso's hoop fell hissing. It encircled both
of us. We were tightly pinned together, and I heard Soup
recite a plaintive little poem:

"Oh no."

Yet there we were, helplessly and snugly surrounded by
Soup's hoop, with an old rope snaking upward, ending in
the clenched fists of the meanest kid in our solar system
. . . Janice Riker, the inhuman replica of Tyrannosaurus
Regina. Whenever old Janice would lose a tooth (or knock
out somebody else's) she'd take the tooth home, stuff it full
of sugar, and watch it ache.

"Rob," said Soup, "we gotta do something."

"Right," I said, "so start thinking and fast. We need one of your brainstorm ideas, quick. One that'll get us *out* of trouble instead of into it."

Somehow, perhaps due to our struggling, the hoop had settled down around our chests and arms. Facing each other, we knew our situation had become dourly desperate. And above, Janice appeared to be preparing to jump.

"Pull," whispered Soup.

"What?"

"Rob, our only hope is to catch Janice by surprise."

"And maybe yank her off the roof?"

"Right."

We could not, however, yank even a little tug or two. Nor could we run in unison, because of the position we were in, belly to belly. I heard a *thud.* The earth trembled. Had a giant meteor hit our planet? No.

Janice had landed.

"Ahhhhhh," she growled with a throat that must have repeatedly gargled with gravel, "I sure got youse two birds. Right where I wantcha. Alive! It ain't no fun to torture the dead."

Torture?

Her word was echoing hauntingly in my brain. Of course Janice would torture us. Considering all my past brushes with the charms of Janice Riker, I certain had little cause to expect candy or flowers.

Janice looked around at the ground. "Okay, youse guys, git your noses open. You'll snuff up a visitor as soon as I find a big enough bug."

Her back was turned.

"Rob," whispered Soup, "now's our chance. You run backward and I'll run forward. Maybe we can break away."

"Okay."

Janice was still searching under some overturned rocks for an appropriate insect, one that might favor a nasal excursion.

"On the count of three," Soup whispered. "Ready?"

I nodded.

"One . . . two . . . *three.*"

We ran. I scrambled backward and Soup, facing me, charged forward. It wasn't what you'd call speedy, but we gained some ground, even though our kneecaps were knocking together like castanets. The rope Janice was holding became rigid and hummed like a low-pitch banjo string.

Janice looked up and saw us. "Hey!" She was holding a large black bug, not quite the size of a Shetland pony. For a moment I thought I heard the bug screaming in terror.

"Faster," said Soup. "Maybe we can snap that old rope, get out from inside this stupid hoop, and head for freedom."

We increased our speed.

Fortune luckily smiled our way. In panic, Janice dropped both the bug and the rope.

"Come back here," she snarled.

Backing up, I couldn't see where Soup and I were going. Yet I didn't care . . . as long as we *went.* Any direction, any point on the compass, was all right with me, as long as it wasn't toward any of Janice Riker's eighty-four knuckles. But not brass knuckles. Janice's were harder.

Over Soup's shoulder, I could see Janice making a diving grab for the rope. Fortunately it eluded her clumsy fingers. She paused for a second or two to recapture the bug that was probable more eager to escape than we were. Janice was even feared by her pet scorpion.

"Keep going," Soup was urging.

I kept going. There were now boards beneath my feet. We were on some sort of a wooden ramp, and I started to smell a very pungent odor. But I kept running backward. The smell wasn't as bad as Janice's breath. In my panic, I'd forgotten that early May was sheepshearing time. All the wool is removed. Then, before being turned loose again, the sheep are bathed to prevent their being bothered by countless ticks and mites that are so harmfully pestering.

Backing up, I was running down a ramp, out of control. All I could see was the old frayed rope snapping. We were free! But then I heard Soup holler.

"Stop!"

Too late. I couldn't stop.

Into the sheep tank we plunged. All three of us. Soup, me, and the hoop. My head went briefly under and so did my pal's. If the liquid we were dunking in smelled awful, it tasted worse. I knew what we had splashed into. The worst-smelling liquid in the world.

Sheep dip.

Two

"Holland," said Miss Kelly.

In school, that May morning, our class had been quickly divided by our teacher. There were twenty-eight of us. Twenty-six children sat on the regular two-seater benches, while Soup and I (still fragrant with sheep dip) were seated apart from the others, next to an open window.

As Miss Kelly was saying something about a dull place called Holland, I glanced halfheartedly at the open book before me, *Frontiers of Geography*. Although the map of South America in my book was certainly colorful, to me it seemed somewhat incomplete.

There was no Holland. Never trust a textbook cartographer.

"As you know, class," Miss Kelly went on to say, "Holland is well known for her colorful tulips, windmills, and something we all like to put in our mouths."

"Tobacco," said Janice, shifting her bulging cud of Bull Durham to the opposite cheek.

"Not exactly," said Miss Kelly with a worn expression of futility. She eyed the near-empty bottle of Anacin on her desk, as if tempted. "Holland," she said, "is famous for . . . *cheese.*"

"Yummm," we sighed with rapt appreciation.

"Some of the cheeses of Holland are rather bland," Miss Kelly added. "Others, however, have a very strong and unpleasant odor."

Twenty-six kids looked over at Soup and me. Several of them pinched their noses. Janice shot us a victorious sneer.

During our teacher's lecture on Holland, I wasn't totally concentrating on *Frontiers of Geography.* Instead, I was observing more alluring topography, the contours of Norma Jean Bissell. Even though Norma Jean sat twenty feet away, her configurations were close enough to measure silently and fervently revere.

"Europe," said Miss Kelly, as I pretended to be entranced with Argentina, "is composed of many small countries. So, in order that we absorb a variety of European cultures, we shall study each little country, one by one. For example, you will be visiting our Learning Free Library, in teams of two pupils each, and devote your attentions to any European country of your own choosing."

I sighed, hoping we might study Samoa.

If given a choice, I would have devoted my entire exploratory life to Norma Jean Bissell, even though Norma Jean had, in the past, pointed out that I smelled of *cow*. Well, she couldn't honestly say that today.

"Pretzelstein," said Miss Kelly, as the tip of her ruler touched some boring little spot on our wall map. "Within the next few days, you'll be allowed to use a collection of magazines at our village library. This helpful magazine is called the *National Geographic*."

Norma Jean Bissell was touching her hair, with a gesture that only a ballerina could have so gracefully employed. I slowly exhaled. If only I could caress Norma Jean's locks. Once I had even dreamed of planting a kiss, ever so lightly, upon her dappled cheek. I was awed by my own imaginary boldness. Yet it was May, spring, and the dormant saps of winterset had begun to gusher upward into veritable torrents of emotional enthusiasm.

I was one of the saps.

". . . and the *National Geographic*," our teacher droned on to say, "will open the distant doors of global adventure . . ."

In order to dismiss any suspicions that Miss Kelly might entertain, concerning my attentiveness regarding Europe, I faked some interest in Brazil. Yet my vision continued to stray, hoping that perhaps Norma Jean Bissell's eyes would tear away from Bolivia (or Europe in general) and glance my way, knowing that my own eyes had ceased to be beacons in academic darkness, and had become limpid pools of longing, dewy with devotion.

Norma Jean, I realized after once having been rewarded with one whiff of her, did *not* smell of sheep dip. Her fragrance was pink, lyrical . . . and *all girl.*

Outside, a car honked.

Miss Kelly looked toward the window, and then smiled. "Class," she said, "I do believe that we are about to entertain a visitor."

The school door opened, without even half a knock, and our one-room school was rewarded with triumphal entry. In marched Miss Boland, our extra-large county nurse, dressed completely in so white and so boiled a uniform that the entire room appeared, by comparison, to be soiled beyond soaping.

Miss Boland, in addition to being our school medic, and in charge of every activity in town, was also a very close friend of Miss Kelly's. They attended church together, every Sunday.

"Gang," she announced, "we've had it."

The expression on Miss Boland's chubby face was hardly one of exuberance. Instead, it was a look of despair.

"Trouble?" asked Miss Kelly.

Miss Boland sighed. "The worst. I just came from Doc Callum's office. That's where I took poor Shorty Smith."

Right then, I looked over at Soup and he stared right back at me, because both of us certain knew who Shorty Smith was. There was hardly a solitary soul in the entire town of Learning who didn't know Shorty. He was our center.

"What's the matter with Shorty?" Miss Kelly asked.

With a futile gesture, Miss Boland sadly shook her head, on which perched a white nurse's cap. "Shorty Smith was working on the construction job, over at the high school . . . and he fell and sprained his ankle."

"This," whispered Soup, "could narrow our chances."

The problem, Soup and I already knew, began last February. We had three snowstorms and had to cancel the final basketball game against Pratt Falls.

"So," said Miss Boland, "our men will have to play without Shorty Smith."

"Well," said Miss Kelly, "I suppose, even though it's May, the make-up game still has to be played." She took a step closer to where Miss Boland stood. "Is there any chance that Shorty's ankle can mend by Saturday?"

Miss Boland made a face.

"Not a prayer. His ankle's all swollen. Looks like somebody inflated it at the filling station air pump. I guess a victory is beyond our reach." Miss Boland forced a smile. "However, I'll still hang some colorful streamers around the gym. And, soon as the game ends, we'll light up the sparklers. The kids'll love that."

"Oh," asked Miss Kelly, "did the box of fireworks come, the ones you ordered for July?"

Miss Boland nodded. "All here. They're safe in a box over at the high school. Yet it won't be much of a celebration. Not without Shorty Smith on the team."

"It seems," Miss Kelly said, "as though Learning will have to locate a substitute, and jolly quick."

"Centers," said Miss Boland, "aren't so simple to find."

"However," said Miss Boland, "nobody could honestly admit that Shorty was tall. I've heard that he is an inch shy of five feet."

"You're right," Miss Boland agreed. "Shorty Smith is our tallest basketball player. He is at least an inch taller than Shorty Pierce or Shorty Lynch, and a good two inches taller than either Shorty Fenner or that stump of a Shorty Merrill."

Soup leaned an inch or two closer to where I sat. Wow, he sure had himself a foul smell.

"Rob," he whispered, "it certain is a shame that you and I can't try out for the town basketball team. We're not short enough."

I giggled.

Yet what Soup was saying was in a way true. None of our Learning basketball players were tall. In fact, as luck would have it, every fellow on our home team had the same nickname:

Shorty.

To make things even worse, all of the Pratt Falls players also shared the same nickname. Stretch. Their captain, Stretch Millerton, was about a yardstick taller than our center, Shorty Smith. In spite of his limited stature, Shorty Smith was nevertheless our *star player.* Was! Needless to say, nobody in Learning could expect Shorty to lope (or limp) around on a basketball court while hobbled by an ankle sprain. Even without a sprained ankle, Shorty was slow enough. If he ran any slower, he'd be in reverse. Yet we all recalled how he'd actual scored four points in one season.

"Well," I said, "there doesn't seem to be much hope of our winning the final game, come Saturday."

Soup looked at me with a sly smirk. "Rob, old top, shame on you. There's always some sort of a way to win a game."

"Not this game."

He shook his head. "Wrong. And it's up to us to invent a way. We ought to start hatching up the wildest device of our lives."

"No," I hissed.

Soup's crazy ideas, I had earlier concluded, were little but roads to ruin, or punishment, and I wanted no part in whatever scheme had seeped into Soup's brain. But I had to hand it to my pal. He was no quitter. Luther Wesley Vinson would never throw in the towel.

He'd sell it.

Only last week I had a really crazy dream. A nightmare. Soup and I had been captured by a band of masked bandits, all of them big and hairy. And there we were, shackled with heavy chains, handcuffs, and leg-irons, side by side with our backs to a damp dungeon wall. We couldn't move. Not even twitch an eyebrow.

Below us was a pit full of sharks and alligators. To make matters worse, our prison cell had no windows, no door, and was fifty yards high. The walls were three feet thick. I was about ready to give up and die, until I heard Soup Vinson's idiotic laugh.

"Now," he chuckled, "here's my plan."

Three

"Ah . . . ahhh . . . ahhh-choooo!"

Soup and I, his battered hoop rolling between us, were on our way home from school. As we were passing by the sheep sheds, we heard the sneeze.

Turning, we saw a man sneeze again.

"God bless you," said Soup.

"Thanks." The man smiled. He wiped his eyes and nose with a red bandanna. "My nostrils can always tell when it's sheep shearing time. Guess I'm allergic to fresh wool."

The gentleman was a stranger to me. In our little town of Learning, everyone knew everybody.

"Mister," I asked, "are you new in town?"

He nodded. "Yup. My name is Murphy. I just came here

to Learning for an hour or so to find out if the basketball game was still on for this coming Saturday night. So I paid a friendly call on Coach Beefjerky."

Soup said, "Sir, you must be from Pratt Falls."

The man smiled. "Right. And I'm doggone glad we don't have any sheep up to Pratt Falls, because *wool fever* makes me sneeze worse'n hay fever. Every single soul in my family's allergic to wool. All us Murphys. And my wife's family suffers the same allergy. Her maiden name was Millerton. Wool just seems to make a Murphy or a Millerton sneeze his head off."

Folding and pocketing his bandanna, Mr. Murphy sneezed once again, climbed into the cab of his truck, and chugged away from town. Even his truck's exhaust sneezed.

Soup and I watched some men shearing sheep for a few minutes. The fresh wool was gradually piling up into a high heap. Then we started up Dugan's Hill, heading for home.

Needless to say, we couldn't roll Soup's hoop *up* Dugan's Hill. It was too steep. So we took turns carrying it. One thing for certain, we wouldn't roll it down Dugan's Hill again, into the unseen talons of Janice Riker. Around the hoop, where her rotten old rope had broken, short lengths were still attached, like a ragged skirt.

As I held the hoop over my head, in fun, the rope fringe dangled from several places on the hoop's rim.

"Hey," said Soup, "it's a basket!"

We raced home.

In a matter of minutes, the two of us were high up on a ladder, nailing the flat hoop to the slide of Soup's barn, which sat close to the dirt road. We tried to hoist it about as high as the baskets at the high school gym. It was the only basketball court in town.

"There," said Soup, pounding in the final nail, "we've got ourselfs a basket for basketball."

"Now all we need is a ball."

Obviously, a baseball wouldn't do. Far too small. And the old black bowling ball that we'd found at The Dump proved to be too heavy. Neither of us could begin to throw it up as high as the hoop.

Soup snapped his fingers.

"I got it."

He disappeared inside his mother's food-storage shed, next to the milk house, and returned carrying a very large vegetable.

It was a cabbage.

The cabbage worked fine for a while, yet it seemed to have one cardinal drawback. As its floppy old leaves kept falling off, one by one, our cabbage got smaller and smaller. Soup looked at it with a bit of disappointment.

"It's not a cabbage anymore," he said.

"No," I said, "it's a brussels sprout. Or a pea."

Looking down at all of the torn and tattered cabbage leaves beneath our hoop, Soup said, "Rob, what we have here isn't a basketball court. It's more like a salad. Or a green rug."

A truck stopped.

As the May afternoon had become fairly warm, the truck's windows had been rolled down, and I heard a radio playing music. The repair truck was small, all white. It was a truck I'd seen many times. Lettering on its flank boldly announced whose truck it was:

BRAUNSCHWEIGER BROTHERS
janitor and plumber

Everybody in town knew the Braunschweiger twins, Boris and Lavoris. They were easily identified, as they were both very small men who always wore identical white coveralls. The back of one coverall said Boris; the other, Lavoris. Being rather senior in age, each Braunschweiger possessed a head of thick gray hair. Both men always needed a haircut.

On this day, however, as their repair truck stopped near Soup's roadside barn, neither Boris nor Lavoris was behind the wheel. In fact, only *one* person was in the truck. Little did Soup and I know that today we'd get quite a surprise. Out of the truck climbed a young man we'd never seen before. The driver wasn't short like Boris and Lavoris.

He was seven feet tall!

"Hooperdunken," he said, a broad and friendly smile spreading across his pleasant face.

Soup and I stared at each other, shrugged our ignorance, then looked again at the stranger. I liked him right away.

He pointed at himself. "Piff." He paused. *"Ich izt* Piffle Shootensinker." Then, gesturing at our basket, he repeated his first word. *"Hooperdunken."* Without another word, the tall fellow turned to his trunk, and took out a round orange object. It wasn't what I expected to see emerging from a repair truck.

"Wow," said Soup, "it's a basketball."

"And a good one," I said.

Without another word, the tall stranger took a shot at our basket. He missed. And then something unusual happened. His face, which had been quite happy, now appeared to become rather sad. The smile melted away into sorrow.

Piff let out a forlorn sigh. *"Mein hooperdunken izt no goot stinken. Ich missen der hooper."*

"He's from out of town," Soup said.

Soup retrieved the basketball, then approached the tall fellow and handed it to him. "Sir," he said, "my name is Luther Vinson, but folks hereabouts all call me Soup." He pointed at me. "This here is my pal, Rob Peck."

"Howdy," I said. Pointing at myself, I said "Rob" again, so he'd understand.

He did. He pointed at Soup and said "Soup," at me and said "Rob," and then at himself. "Piffle Shootensinker."

"Where are you from?" Soup asked. "Are you from Germany? Austria? Maybe you hail from Switzerland . . . or Holland."

"*Nein,*" he said. "Pretzelstein."

Soup looked at me. "Rob, that's in Europe. Today, in school, Miss Kelly was talking about it. It's a tiny little country."

"Pretzelstein?" I asked.

"*Jah,*" said Piffle, standing very tall and even more proudly. "*Ich izt a Pretzelsteiner.*"

Just then, from a distance, a sheep made its usual bleat. *Baa.* The noise of the sheep seemed to make Piffle Shootensinker look even sadder. He brushed away a tear.

"Maybe he's homesick," said Soup.

"*Jah,*" he said. "*Homesicken. Ich missen mein sheepen.*" Pulling out his wallet, Piffle fumbled for a small photograph, which he showed to Soup and me. "*Zee?*" he asked. The photo was a picture of Piff standing among a flock of sheep. Piffle sniffled. "*Missen mein sheepen.*"

"He misses his sheep," said Soup.

Piffle Shootensinker showed us a second photograph, one that featured a very large and shaggy dog. "*Dot,*" said Piffle, "*izt mein sheependag* . . . Adolph." The dog seemed to be able to stand on its hind legs.

"His sheepdog," I said.

"Right," said Soup. "In a few minutes, if we talk to our

new friend Piffle, we'll be able to speak Pretzelsteiner too." Soup pointed at Piff's basketball, then up at the makeshift basket we'd nailed to the barn. "Try another, Piff."

Piffle shot again . . . and missed. Badly.

"Maybe," said Soup, "old Piff didn't play any basketball back home in Pretzelstein. On that last shot, he missed hitting the hoop by a good eight feet. But he's twice the height of any of the men on our Learning team."

Stretching my neck, and looking up up up at Piffle's face, I said, "That's a lowdown shame. He sure is tall enough, but he just can't shoot a basket."

I tried it.

Much to my surprise, I actual did sink a basket on my fourteenth attempt. Soup sunk one on his eleventh.

"Goot," said Piffle.

He tried again and again. Yet every one of his shots somehow went wide or long. Or didn't even hit the barn! Tall as he was, Mr. Piffle Shootensinker just wasn't much of a basketballer, even though his name suggested the contrary.

Piff's face looked more sorrowful and more homesick than it had earlier. But then something happened! It was his truck's radio. A very weird kind of music started to play. To my ear, it was hardly music at all. More like indigestion. Yet to the ears of the tall stranger from Pretzelstein, the wacky music suddenly seemed to brighten his expression. He pointed at the radio, cupped a hand to his ear, and danced a little joyful jig.

Then . . .

From a distance of at least thirty feet, Mr. Piffle Shootensinker fired the basketball. Up it went, higher, farther, and . . . *whoosh.* A basket! He did it again, this time using his left hand. Another basket. He couldn't miss.

Happily he danced again to the gurgling music.

"Spitzentootle," he said.

Soup and I looked at each other.

Spitzentootle?

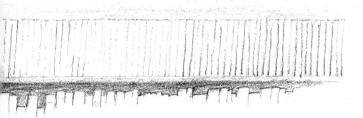

Four

"Bull's-eye," said Soup. "There they are."

Soup was right. There they all were, stacked upright on a tidy row, high on a shelf above our heads. I could identify them by their yellow spines.

A week or so ago, all of them had been on a lower shelf, within our reach. Mrs. Spinnerford had apparently moved them. Perhaps because she had caught Soup and me peeking at some of the more exotic pictures. The unclad ladies of Samoa.

"Rob," said Soup, "I'll have to stand on your back. So be a good fellow and bend over."

"But you're a bit huskier than I am," I said. "Why don't I stand on you?"

"Ah," said Soup, "for good reason. Because I'm the one who always remembers which issues have the most revealing photographs."

I sighed.

It was useless, I knew, to argue with Luther Wesley Vinson. So, abandoning further protest, I bent over, allowing my pal to leap lightly upon my back. Pacing to and fro along my backbone, Soup was making his unhurried selection.

"Eureka," he said at last.

"Did you find it?" I grunted, still bending over, arms straight, hands braced to my knees. "It doesn't have to be Samoa. Just grab a few magazines and climb down."

Soup finally dismounted.

Half a minute later, the two of us sat at one of the reading tables at the Learning Free Library, thumbing through an issue of the *National Geographic.* My spine was still a bit sore, yet the discomfort was being erased by my anticipation of an intimate glimpse of South Pacific femininity. Closing my eyes, I halfway expected to hear the strumming of a ukulele.

Instead, I heard a voice, one that did not sing. Nor was it the voice of a pretty young girl.

"You," said Mrs. Spinnerford, who looked nothing at all like a slender, brown-skinned beauty.

Looking up, eyes now open, I saw our village librarian, and the scowl on her sober face seemed to betray her feelings about young boys and their interest in Samoan girls.

"Luther Vinson and Robert Peck," she whispered, hissing like an adder, "you both have been warned about your habitual misuse of the *National Geographic.*"

Soup slyly flipped to an entirely different section of the magazine. Glancing down, I couldn't see any photos of the girls of Samoa. Instead, I saw only knees. Naked knees! Men in short pants and suspenders, holding tulips, and eating cheese. On the opposite page, however, was a flock of sheep. I blinked. My eyes couldn't accept what I saw.

"As you can see, Mrs. Spinnerford," said Soup. "we aren't looking at what you told us to avoid. We're doing a project for school, just the way Miss Kelly assigned."

Mentioning our teacher's name, Soup always claimed, was a sure way to add her dignity to his deviltry. The name of Miss Kelly always frosted the cake of mischief with an icing of scholarly clout.

I couldn't tear my eyes from the page in *National Geographic.* Why not? Because our sudden good fortune just wasn't to be believed. The jackpot! There it was, boldly printed across the entire double page.

PRETZELSTEIN

I looked up, and smiled. "That's the honest truth, Mrs. Spinnerford," I said quickly. "Miss Kelly told us to pair up and prepare something about a country." Soup looked at me with curiosity. My finger tapped the open pages of the magazine. "And," I said, "we chose Pretzelstein."

My pal looked down, and grinned. "Right," he said. "That's our country. It's in Europe."

Even though I was about to add that I'd been thinking it was somewhere in South America, I decided to keep silent. Peering over her bifocal glasses, Mrs. Spinnerford seemed to be performing an impossible feat. Standing before us, she actual read *Pretzenstein* upside down.

"Pretzelstein?" she whispered.

We nodded.

Mrs. Spinnerford smiled. "Good," she said. "I was wrong, presuming that your interests were closer to Samoa. You may continue your studies."

As our librarian marched away, having staunchly preserved Vermont virtue, Soup and I looked at the magazine, then at each other, and grinned.

"Rob," he said, "that was a bolt of slippery thinking. I'm proud of you, weasel. Someday you'll be a lawyer."

"It was luck," I admitted. "Yet here it is, everything we'll possible need for our homework assignment. And what's *not* in this article, we'll ask our new friend about."

"So we shall," Soup said. "Mr. Piffle Shootensinker knows everything about Pretzelstein."

We read.

Page upon page, complete with pictures aplenty in color, Soup and I sponged up Pretzelsteiner facts galore. It, we learned, was the smallest country in Europe. Snugly nestled in the Bavarian Alps, it was renowned for sheep, music, and basketball.

"Here it is," Soup whispered. Then he read aloud. "Pretzelsteiner history is rife with famous people, one of whom was Baron Wolfgang Piddlehopper Von Spitzen, inventor of the most popular musical instrument in Pretzelstein."

Soup stopped reading.

"Well," I asked, "what is it? Which musical instrument did Baron Von Spitzen invent?"

"The *spitzentootle.*"

"Honest?"

I stared at the text in *National Geographic.* Sure enough, there it was. And more. Wolfgang Piddlehopper Von Spitzen created his instrument for one purpose . . . to encourage his basketball team to *win.*

After turning another page, Soup pointed to a photograph. I looked. There it was, a picture of a genuine *spitzentootle,* or so the caption read. The instrument itself didn't look like anything I'd ever seen before. More like a machine with tubes and pipes. Yet it could produce music. This we knew, because Piffle Shootensinker's truck radio had played a *spitzentootle* solo.

"Rob," said Soup, as his elbow met my ribs to capture my attention, "just listen to this." He read: "Baron Wolfgang Piddlehopper Von Spitzen used to brag that whenever a *spitzentootle* was playing, during a *hooperdunken* game, the Pretzelsteiner players couldn't miss a shot. This was why the basketballers from the little Duchy of Pretzelstein were considered the premier team of Europe."

The article also stated that the Baron's team turned professional and toured the world, billing themselves as the Pretzelsteiner Globe Trotters.

We turned a page.

Wool, according to the *National Geographic,* was the principal export of Pretzelstein. Pictured again was a flock of sheep. Plus some information about an ailment caused by wool, an allergy called *sheepensneezer.* On the opposing page, a photograph of a sheepdog. Staring at the dog's picture, I felt a chill run up and down my spine, like a frightened xylophone. The Pretzelsteiner *sheependag* reminded me of something, or of someone, yet I couldn't quite place who.

"Wow," said Soup, "that sheepdog sort of looks like somebody we know. What do you think?"

Nodding, I silently agreed.

"And it isn't another dog," I said under my breath, too jittery to utter the truth.

Soup suddenly snapped his fingers. "Rob, old top, a thought just struck me."

"Did it hurt?"

"No," said Soup. "Not a bit. In fact, it feels mighty good. Because I've got an idea that just might help our Learning team win the basketball game against Pratt Falls. I'm glad we told Miss Boland about the new guy in town. Piffle is part of my scheme."

I shuddered.

Little did I know that my best pal, Luther Wesley Vinson, was about to say that quartet of horrifying words of my recent nightmare. But then he said them, all four, causing me to accept the awful truth. My bad dream was becoming real.

"Now here's my plan."

Five

"This is it," said Soup.

After evening chores, and supper, the two of us had met at Soup's house.

Out back.

He was bending over outside a small window, one that led into their cellar. The window was very dirty, coated with dust, as though it hadn't been opened in at least fifty or sixty years. It was a foot or so below the ground. In a pit.

"Doggone the luck," said Soup.

"What's the matter?"

"It's locked."

His fingers pushed on the frame.

"Maybe," I said, "if we both push . . ."

"Okay."

We pushed.

Nothing happened. But then we pushed a grunt or two harder, and I felt the old window give a little.

"Hey," said Soup, "it's coming loose."

Again we pushed.

Making a creaky noise, the little window slowly opened, swinging upward on a pair of rusty hinges. Inside, it was dark. Pitch-black. Many times I'd been down in Soup Vinson's cellar, yet not in this secret part. Right now, I didn't hanker to go.

"Rob, did you bring the flashlight?"

"Yup."

Our flashlight wasn't a very good one. Soup and I had gotten it for free. It had taken us about a century (well, at least a year) to suffer the torture of gagging down our countless bowls of Soppies, a breakfast cereal.

Soppies didn't snap, crackle, or pop.

They would only listlessly lie in the bottom of a cereal bowl, sop up the milk, and create an instant oaty sludge fit only to be eaten by losers. Or starving maggots. Twenty-eight box tops later, we'd sent away for the flashlight, one called *Prowler's Pal*.

"Rob, you go first."

"Not me. It's your house. You know your own cellar a lot better than I do."

"To be honest about it," Soup said, "I've never been down in there. Not even once. But the hour has come."

"What's down there that we need?"

"You'll find out, old top." He smiled. "Now, if you go first, I'll tell you a real funny story about what happened here, years and years ago."

"Well . . . okay."

"Here's a clue," Soup said. "When we moved here, my folks located only *part* of a cellar. But we think there's a room down here they couldn't find. A secret room. So we're finding it."

"We're looking for a *room*?"

"No, not exactly. What we're in search of, down in the darkness, begins with *M.*"

As he talked, Soup was holding the flashlight in one hand and helping me through the window with the other.

As I backed into the small window, there didn't seem to be anything to stand on. Soup was holding on to both of my wrists, as I was holding his.

"Don't drop me," I said. "Whatever you do, Soup . . . *don't let go.*"

He let go.

"Oops," I heard Soup say as I fell.

Falling into darkness isn't a whole bunch of fun. I landed, however, on both feet. The earth beneath me was soft. The air seemed to be very damp, almost as if I was under water, instead of under a house.

"I'm here," I whispered to Soup. "So tell me your funny story." I blinked in the darkness. "And it better be dog-gone funny."

Soup's head poked in above me.

"Well," he said, "there are two kinds of *funny*. There's the ha-ha funny, and then there's the other kind . . . the *weird* funny. And, years ago, an old lady who lived in this house, Mrs. Murdock, stabbed her husband to death with a kitchen knife. The story goes that she killed him somewhere in our cellar. The funny part, however, was her poor husband's name."

Soup paused.

"Well," I said, my voice echoing in the blackness of the cellar, "what was his name?"

"Lucky Murdock."

A sudden chill swept over me, as though I was no longer a boy. Instead, a clam.

"Soup," I said, "you'd better get down here, and quick, or I'm coming back up. But first, toss me the flashlight."

He tossed it. I caught it.

A spiderweb touched my face. Quickly I flashed the feeble light from *Prowler's Pal* into the web. Sure enough, there was a spider. A large one. But he seemed to be deader than Lucky Murdock.

"Come on, Soup."

"Is there room?"

"Plenty."

Down he came. He landed near me.

"Now," he said, "all we do is find that old Murdock thing."

"The *knife*?" A chill went up and down my spine like a frightened elevator. It felt like I was wearing a wet shirt.

"No," said Soup, "the Melodeo."

"What in heck is a Melodeo?"

Soup slowly sighed.

"An instrument. A Melodeo is merely a proper name, a particular brand of melodeon. And a melodeon is a small organ. Robert, you try my patience at times, with your lack of artistic culture." He clapped a hand on my shoulder, sending dust flying into the darkness. "However," he said, "soon we may sponsor your musical debut."

"My *what*?"

"Nothing. Don't worry, it won't hurt."

Dust seemed to be lurking everywhere down in Soup's cellar. It made me sneeze. Soup sneezed too.

"Sheepensneezer," he said. "But down here there aren't any sheep. Only spiders. Maybe we're *lucky*."

"Don't," I said, "use that word."

"Rob, like the good fellow you are, shine your flashlight over in the corner . . . ah, that's excellent. There's something there."

I prayed it wasn't Lucky Murdock. And then prayed even harder that it wouldn't be his merry widow with her flashing blade.

Closing my eyes, I asked Soup Vinson a question. "What is it?"

"Rob, old sport, I do believe that you and I are in fortune. Yes! We possible hit the proverbial Pot of Jack." Soup pointed. "Behold!"

Squinting in the damp darkness (or dark dampness), I looked where *Prowler's Pal* was shining its soppy beam.

I saw a pair of black eyes.

A rat went scurrying away into darker regions of the Vinson cellar. I don't like spiders that much. Not at all. Yet a spider isn't as scary as a rat the size of a golden retriever. A kid could have throwed a saddle on that rat and rode it to school.

"It's a rat," I said.

"Rob," said Soup, "forget the rat. *Look!* See what our friendly rat was sitting on."

I looked.

It didn't appear at all familiar.

"What is it?"

My pal moved toward it.

"Ah," he said, "I was right."

"Well?"

"Rob, old tiger, we may have discovered something important . . . a milestone in the motivation of crime."

Through the gloom, Soup and I inched forward, as if we suddenly had become Vermont's answer to Dr. Watson and Sherlock Holmes.

"There it is," said Soup.

Sure enough, there it was.

Our feeble Soppies flashlight, complete with two F batteries, was casting a circle around a large box.

Soup's hand brushed off some dust.

"Here," he whispered.

I squinted. "It's an *M.*"

As he continued to scatter dust, more letters loomed into view. Seven letters in all.

MELODEO.

"Rob, this is the first step of what could become our master plan . . . one that'll help our town basketball team win Saturday's big game."

Moving closer, I felt *Prowler's Pal* trembling in my hand.

"You're right," I told Soup. "This Melodeo is some sort of a musical instrument. All of these black and white things are a keyboard. Sort of like a piano. Without as many keys."

For almost a minute, Soup Vinson remained very quiet. Looking up at the tiny window we'd crawled through, then down at the old dusty melodeon, he seemed to be in deep thought.

"Rob, old sport, we have a small problem. In fact, the problem might be too small."

"What's the problem?"

"Well, it's this. How are we going to lift this Melodeo and shove it through that little window up there?"

"We can't."

"You're correct. We can't. So, our only solution is to take only the keys, and leave the rest of the melodeon down here in the cellar."

"Okay by me," I said.

Soup had brought a small screwdriver. And it fitted the two screws. We loosened the entire keyboard (only twenty-six keys) and shoved it up and through the tiny window.

"There," Soup said.

"Let's get out of here, Soup. I don't like it down here in this secret cellar of yours. I keep thinking about the knife, and what happened to poor Mr. Murdock. How come Mrs. Murdock stabbed her husband with a kitchen knife?"

Moving a barrel and a couple of old boxes, we stood higher, and climbed up and out of the secret cellar.

"Well," said Soup, "I'll tell you what my guess is. She stabbed him because she went nuts. She couldn't stand the awful way he played his Melodeo."

"What was so bad about it? What did his Melodeo music sound like?"

Soup grinned.

"Like a *spitzentootle.*"

Six

"Twenty-six keys," said Soup.

I looked at them, as the two of us sat with our backs leaning against the side of Soup's chicken coop. Some of the keys were black. Most of them, however, were white, yet the white keys had turned a bit yellow.

"We can't leave our melodeon keys lying around loose," said Soup. "Too many grown-ups get too curious and then start asking a bunch of troublesome questions."

"Let's hide 'em."

"Good idea," he said.

We stashed our borrowed keyboard keys in a safe place, in a nook in Soup's cow shed, behind an old canvas tarpaulin.

"That," said Soup, "is that."

Yawning, I admitted how sleepy I was, said so-long to my pal, headed home, apologized for being a minute late (as I was always ordered to be home by dark), and crawled into my bed.

My dream, like many of my dreams whether awake or asleep, was filled with pastoral images of Norma Jean Bissell.

There she was, gowned in a pale pink organdy, extravagant with lace. My pretty princess was beckoning to me from the ivy-covered balcony of her castle. Oddly enough, the castle resembled a large Melodeo.

I dismounted from my white horse.

Climbing up an ivy vine (poison ivy) I passed a basketball rim. A large cabbage was stuck in the hoop. Below, some sheep were grazing and somebody was sneezing. Closer and closer to Norma Jean Bissell I climbed. On her head was a crown, a gold and silver tiara, with EAT AT JOE'S spelled out in rubies and emeralds.

She was chewing.

"What are you eating?" I asked her.

"Pretzels. Want one?"

"Thanks." I bit into one of Norma Jean's gray pretzels. It tasted like wool. As I looked into her eyes, she didn't seem to be Norma Jean Bissell anymore. She was an older lady.

"Who are you?" I asked.

She scowled at me. "Mrs. Murdock. Do you mind if I

marry you and call you Lucky?" As the strange lady asked the question, she held up a large basketball, which she then stabbed with a kitchen knife.

BAM.

The ball exploded. In fright, and leaning backward, I realized that I was falling. Down, down . . . until I splashed into the castle's moat, which was filled with sheep dip. The lifeguard, who turned out to be Miss Boland, saved me from drowning. Some *spitzentootle* music was playing.

Miss Boland said, "Welcome to Pretzelstein."

I heard another voice. Soup's.

"Rob," he said.

"Go away," I told him. "Because I don't want either you or Mrs. Murdock here in my dream. I want Norma Jean."

"Rob . . . wake up."

I woke.

Leaving my bed, I staggered to my open bedroom window. Below, down on the ground, was Luther Wesley Vinson. Beside him lay our keyboard.

"Rob, get dressed. I need your help."

"It's the middle of the night."

"But I just planned it all out. We don't have much time, so hurry up."

"Now?"

Soup nodded. "You won't believe my idea. It can't miss. It'll win the basketball game for us, come Saturday."

Why, at midnight, I pulled on a pair of pants and my

sneakers to race into town with Soup Vinson, I'll never be able to explain. It's just one of those crazy things people do when nutty friends wake them up and they're too sleepy to argue. We took our melodeon keys with us.

Once in town, Soup pointed.

"There it is."

I blinked in the dark. "There's what?"

"You'll soon see."

Soup raced into a narrow alleyway, between two stores. I followed. At the rear of one of the stores, he stopped.

"This is it," he announced, hiding the keyboard in a nearby hollow tree.

Squinting, I managed to read a slightly crooked sign that hung over the back door of the store:

BRAUNSCHWEIGER BROTHERS
delivery entrance

"Okay," said Soup, approaching several boxes of discarded rubbish, "now we start our serious searching."

"For what?"

"Well, just for starters, we'll need a vacuum cleaner. Hopefully one that still works. Add to that, a variety of plumbing supplies. This is the smartest place to look."

My mind was now working, realizing why we'd come to this place. The Braunschweiger brothers were twins, with two professions. One was a *janitor;* the other, a master *plumber.* So, up to this point in my reasoning, Soup's idea held a modicum of logic.

"Yahoo," Soup yelled.

"Keep your voice down," I warned him. "We can't afford to be caught doing all this. We'd be in a heap of trouble."

Soup grinned. "Rob, don't worry."

As a rule, I seldom worry. Only sometimes. Whenever my pal Soup Vinson tells me I shouldn't . . . then I worry like a wart.

"Why were you saying *yahoo*?"

"Because," said Soup, "here in this trash box, I happened to stumble across a vacuum cleaner."

"How big?"

"Industrial strength."

"Good. What else do we need?"

"Sink plungers. A red rubber cup with a handle. Old ones. The older and softer they are, the better they'll be for our purpose."

As we searched through the rubbish, fortune again smiled in our direction. There they lay, in a pile of refuse, plungers of varying sizes, mostly with broken handles.

"Soup, I found the plungers."

"Great. How many?"

"Looks like a couple of dozen. And they seem to be all different in size."

"Excellent. Rob, old sport, next we need a large galvanized hot-water tank, the kitchen stove variety, and we're almost fully supplied. Except, of course, for an old garden hose."

When it came to my understanding one of Luther Wesley Vinson's contraptions, the more he explained, the less I knew.

"What," I asked him, "does a hot-water tank have to do with a vacuum cleaner and a garden hose?"

Soup winked. "You'll eventually see, my friend. Be a believer. We may not be brainy. But we sure have been lucky."

Lucky!

"Don't," I said, "use that word. Every time you do, I keep remembering poor Mr. Murdock, and I get goose bumps."

Soup's eyes widened.

"Rob, we may have hit another jackpot."

I looked. Yet all I could see in the alley gloom was a clothesline, with clothes hanging, gently luffing in the breeze. Two garments, small and white. Hurrying to the clothesline, Soup touched one of the items. I went too. Now I could see exactly what they were.

"Coveralls," said Soup.

He was right. That's what they were. On the back of one of the white coveralls were letters. With some difficulty I managed to make out the name.

BORIS

The other coverall had a name too. LAVORIS. They obviously belonged to the Braunschweiger twins . . . one a janitor (which explained the vacuum cleaner) and the other a plumber (sink plungers). Soup had to be either very bright or very stupid.

"Rob," he said as he quickly began to remove a clothespin, "we're going to have to borrow these coveralls."

"Why?"

"When the hour arrives, at which time our cleverness ripens and bears fruit, you shall see."

Fruit? The only fruit I could readily identify at that moment was Soup Vinson. And he, obviously, was nuttier than a hickory tree.

"I smell trouble," I said.

"How come?"

"Soup, we can't go wandering around town and borrow everything in sight. Sooner or later, we're certain to be caught, and tossed in the jailhouse, for stealing. Our folks will throw a fit. Neither one of us will be allowed off the farm until our fiftieth birthday."

My pal continued to remove the two coveralls from the clothesline, and these he hid beneath an old wheelbarrow.

"Right now," I told him, "I've got to know now what in the name of stupidity we are doing. None of this stuff has anything to do with winning a basketball game."

"Ah," said Soup, "but it does. All we need now, other than a water tank, a Sterno stove, and a hose, is a sign that reads FREE CANDY."

I sighed. "Is that all? Is it really *all*?"

"And," said Soup, "a jug of molasses."

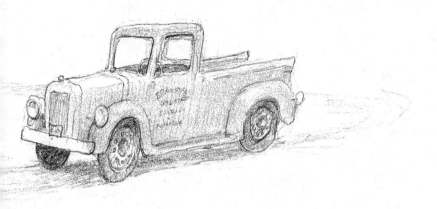

Seven

Soup stopped.

The two of us were walking home from school, and about to pass by the sheepshearing barn. Men were working, the sheep were bleating, a sheepdog was barking. And in the wool bin, the harvested wool was piling up into a modest mountain.

"Right about there," Soup said.

Scratching my head, I said absolutely nothing, in a silent effort to decode whatever it was that Soup Vinson had in mind.

"Rob, I have nifty news."

"Such as?"

"Early this morning, right after feeding the chickens and gathering eggs, I painted our sign. White background with red letters. Its message is two irresistible words."

"Free Candy."

"Right. And nobody in the entire world will be able to resist biting the bait."

"Did you find any rope?"

"Yup." Soup nodded. "I located a whole jug of molasses, plus a sturdy eye-screw for the cork." He turned to me. "And you've got a garden hose."

"I got it. Even though I have no idea what we're going to do with all this stuff, at least we have a hose to water it down."

Soup's face brightened.

"Water," he said. "Maybe, just possible maybe, you've come up with the magic touch." He patted me on the back. "Rob, old sport, you're the beacon of light at the midnight of creativity."

"Thanks," I said, with an honest shrug of total confusion.

We went to Soup's house and used up another cabbage, trying to shoot baskets into the hoop we'd nailed to the barn.

A truck tooted its horn. Not in anger, but merely with a friendly-sounding *beep-beep.* As the Braunschweiger truck pulled to a stop, I recognized its driver. It was Piffle, our seven-foot friend and Learning's latest import from the Duchy of Pretzelstein. Jumping from the truck, he approached us wearing a jovial expression. Then, pointing a finger at himself, he spoke a name.

"Smith."

This confusing outburst caused Soup and me to look at each other. Soup seemed to be as mixed-up as I was.

Piffle's smile broadened, even though speaking English was obviously a difficulty. "Shorty Smith," he said, walking around in a little circle and faking a limp. "Saturday," he said, *"vee do hooperdunken. Ich izt* center."

"Hey," said Soup. "That's really great. Then our nurse, Miss Boland, steered you to Coach Beefjerky, who signed you up for the team." Soup extended his hand. "Congratulations to you, Piff. You're to be Shorty Smith's substitute."

I shook Piff's hand too.

"Good going," I told him. "You can fill Shorty's shoes."

Without another word, Piffle Shootensinker went to his truck, and then reappeared with his basketball. Again he tried to sink a hooker, and missed. The ball fell a mile wide. Piffle's face fell too, into a forlorn expression.

"Stinken," he sighed.

"Don't worry, Piff," said Soup. He ran to retrieve the ball, handing it to its seven-foot owner. "Rob and I have a

plan. We already know you miss your sheep. But this coming Saturday night, you'll be Learning's star player."

"Jah," he said. *"Ich missen* Adolph."

Soup snapped his fingers. His face beamed with inspira-
tion. "That's it, Rob. Our tall friend here misses his sheepdog, his *sheependag,* even more than he's missing the
sheep."

I nodded. "But I don't guess there's anything that either
you or I can do about it."

"Wrong," said Soup.

"What'll we do?"

"Well," he replied, "if we can't send Piffle back to Europe, to Pretzelstein, in order to visit his *sheependag,*
there just might be an outside chance to bring Adolph, his
dog, to the basketball game on Saturday."

Piffle Shootensinker stared down at Soup and me, a look
of confusion clouding his face. For sure, our tall friend
wasn't any more mixed-up than I was. For the past three
days, if Soup Vinson had spoken only in Pretzelsteiner,
instead of English, I couldn't have been more befuddled.

"Piff," I said, straining my neck to look up at his face,
"don't let Soup muddy the water on your brain. I never
even begin to savvy half of whatever Soup's saying. And
far less of what he's thinking. But, believe me, Luther
Wesley Vinson really can think."

Soup grinned.

"Pal," he said to me, "thanks a lot."

"Aw, forget it," I told Soup. "Anybody who claims he can win a basketball game with a garden hose and a sink plunger, has gotta have more between his ears than just molasses."

In a book one time, I'd read that genius is right neighborly with insanity. First cousins. Maybe, I was now considering, Soup really wasn't a genuine genius. Perhaps he was merely nuts.

"Here," said Soup, taking the basketball from Piffle, "let's all practice. Maybe you're just rusty, Piff."

Soup shot a basket.

So did I.

But our lanky Pretzelsteiner couldn't seem to arch his ball within a holler of Soup's hoop. He merely tried, and failed.

"Nein gooten," he said sourly.

"Never mind," Soup told him, "that you're no good. You can be. Piff, you couldn't miss last Monday when your truck radio was playing that *spitzentootle* song."

"Jah," said Piffle, with a weak little nod of his head. *"Ich missen der spitzentootle* too."

Soup turned to me.

"Rob, there's a hurdle in our path."

"Only one?"

"Several," said Soup. As he spoke, he was watching

Piffle trying to make a basket. Trying and failing. "For one thing, I heard that it costs fifty cents admission into the high school gym, to watch the game."

"We don't have fifty cents."

"*Jah,*" said Soup, "to borrow a Pretzelsteiner phrase, seeing as we've already been borrowing everything else. It's true. We don't have it. Yet we momentarily have two white coveralls. And I know where we maybe can find a typewriter."

I gagged. "Typewriter?" I took a deep breath. "Don't tell me. You're planning to pour molasses on a typewriter, whip it with a garden hose, and then offer it under a sign that reads FREE CANDY."

"Not quite," said Soup.

Piffle missed another lay-up. As he'd practiced he hadn't managed to dunk a single shot. His facial expression was a look of despair.

"*Ach,*" said Piffle, "*mein hooperdunken izt uppen der creeken midout ein piddle.*"

"I'll be darned," I said. "Do you folks actual say that in South America too?"

"*Jah,*" he said.

With a wave of his hand, Piffle took his basketball, climbed aboard his truck, and motored away in the direction of town.

Soup and I watched him go.

Turning to me, Soup's face was a study in grim resolution. "A dog and a song," he quietly commented. "That just might be Saturday's winning combination."

"And," I reminded him, "a typewriter. What a relief to know we're finally on track."

"We've been *barken* up *der* wrong *piddle.*"

Eight

"Three," said Soup.

"Three?"

"Right. We use three plans."

The two of us were relaxing on Soup's back porch, after school, inhaling whatever it was that Mrs. Vinson was cooking for supper. It sure smelled *goot.*

As I leaned against a porch post, I couldn't see much of Soup, because he was lying in a hammock. All I could see was his pad and pencil. The pencil was writing, stopping, then erasing, and writing again with a renewed fury.

"Rob," he said, "it's all finished."

"Your new song?"

"Right. But we can't practice singing it here on the

porch. The kitchen window's open, my mother will hear us, and start wondering whatever it is we're up to. She hasn't trusted me since last February."

"How come?"

"Remember when I dumped all those boxes of Jell-O powder into the horse trough and made twenty pounds of frozen cherry dessert, for George Washington's birthday?"

"I remember."

We went out into Soup's barn.

"Okay," said Soup, holding up his piece of paper, "this is it. Our musical masterpiece. And it'll mark the first time that a Vermonter ever wrote a ballad about a duchess."

"What's the title?"

"Mein Pretzelsteiner Gal."

"Catchy."

Soup looked up from his scribble. "Rob, you'd better like it. Because you're the one who's going to have to sing it."

"Me?"

"Right. You want to impress Norma Jean Bissell, don't you? Well, nothing impresses a girl quicker than a love song."

"But I'm not a good singer."

"Rob, you don't have to be. There's no cause for panic. After all, you won't be singing a solo."

"You'll be singing too?"

"Uh, not exactly. But I'll be supplying the rest of the music, that is, if my design holds water. Which reminds me. I know where we can locate a hot-water tank, the big silvery kind."

"Soup," I sighed, as the pair of us arrived at his barn, "maybe we're already in enough hot water. Even without a tank to put it in."

"Rob, old sport, trust me for a few more days, and you'll see how we do three things that are sort of worth doing. First, we cheer up good old Piffle, our newfound friend from Pretzelstein. Second, we get even with Janice Riker. Third, little does she know, but we're intending to recruit Janice's help in order to win the basketball game."

As I slumped onto a bale of hay, I could only groan out one interrogative word.

"How?"

Soup's face brightened. "Ah, that is the secret. Our brilliant secret in common. You're in this too, old buddy."

I gulped. "That's what I'm afraid of. When the two of us wind up in prison, wearing striped suits *and sharing the same cell,* you'll probably look at me, grin, and then happily announce that . . . *we're in this together.*"

Soup grinned at me. "Pals forever."

We practiced Soup's new song. After the first run-through, I had to admit that it wasn't the best song in the world. Perhaps it was the worst. *Mein Pretzelsteiner Gal* wasn't about to win an award for musical talent and it sure wouldn't help me to win the heart of Norma Jean.

"Soup," I asked, "where do I have to sing this doggone song of yours? Why don't *you* sing it?"

"Because," Soup explained, "one of us has to sing and the other fingers the keyboard."

"I could do that."

"Perhaps," said Soup, "and perhaps not. Remember that I'm the one who's had a piano lesson."

"You only had one," I told Soup.

"It was all I needed. But *you* haven't had any. I'll bet you couldn't even find Middle C. Here's a test, Rob. Right now, where is Middle C?"

"I don't know."

Soup pulled a white keyboard from his pocket. "Here," he said. "Here is Middle C." He grinned. "So you sing, and I play the *spitzentootle*."

"Okay," I said. "You win."

Soup said, "It's not the song that's important. What really matters is" . . . Soup giggled . . . "our overall effect. Or perhaps I should say coverall."

Again we sang *Mein Pretzelsteiner Gal*.

To me, the words didn't make a whole lot of sense, because good old Soup had a language all his own. Yet the tune wasn't bad.

"Just you wait," said Soup, "until you hear it with a *spitzentootle* playing in the background."

"I can wait."

"Now," said Soup, "we don't have any time to fritter. There's too much to do."

He paced back and forth inside the barn, a straw twitching impatiently in his mouth. One could easily discern, by his serious expression, that Luther Wesley Vinson was in deep thought.

Suddenly he stopped pacing.

"Janice," he said.

I winced.

There was something about a mention of Janice Riker's name that made me jumpy, and more nervous than a long-tail cat in a roomful of rocking chairs. Soup's plan, I was now concluding, had something to do with our getting close to Janice, a thought that could curdle all the milk I'd swallowed since my weaning.

"I don't like it, Soup."

"Why not?"

"Your plan smells of trouble. It'll maybe get the two of us into sheep dip again. Or into jail. And where Janice Riker is concerned, into the hospital."

"Don't worry," Soup told me. "I got it all figured out. Wait right there."

Soup left.

I waited.

He returned, carrying three objects. A long length of stout twine, an eye-screw of sturdy size, and an earthen molasses jug. As I watched, he loosened the cork. Then, twisting slowly, Soup screwed the eye-screw into the cork, then knotted one end of twine to the eye.

"Watch," he said, giving the twine a yank.

Plook!

Out popped the cork.

Soup smiled. "Now," he said, "if only it'll function like

that when it's upside down." He looked at me. "Rob, do you happen to have a penny?"

Searching my pockets, I found three gum wrappers, some tinfoil, a football valve, one rusty fishhook, two sinkers, a Ty Cobb baseball bubble gum card, and part of a poem that I'd started to compose for Norma Jean Bissell. "Roses are red" was all it said. But then, inside a linty wad of yarn, I located a penny.

"Good," said Soup.

"Why?"

"Because, on Saturday, I'm going to ask you to visit Mr. Jubert's candy counter, and purchase three molasses kisses. As you know, they sell three for a penny."

I didn't question Soup's request. The sacrificing of my only cent seemed meager, considering all the creativity Soup was contributing. So, I reasoned, my one tarnished penny was little enough.

"Tomorrow," said Soup, "we have to construct our molasses trap, and we already know exactly where we're going to put it."

"We do?"

Soup nodded. "Above the wool. And if our good ol' pal Piffle Shootensinker *izt missen* Adolph, *der sheependag,* as much as he admits, Learning's basketball team may have a chance to win over Pratt Falls."

"Makes sense to me," I said, not caring to confess that none of it sounded even slightly reasonable.

Soup, I was now convinced, had stubbed his mental toe, and was now heck-bent for slipping off the deep end. I was hoping we weren't about to embark on another plunge into a bin of sheep dip. Yet such a fragrant fate might be preferable to an encore with Janice.

My years of close association with Soup Vinson warned me that I'd somehow feel better, and worry less, if I didn't fully comprehend what my pal was planning. Not that Soup would readily explain. He seldom did. And, upon those rare occasions, I understood less (following his explanation) than I had before. Had I known, I would have fretted away like a guitar.

Plook!

Soup was busy with the cork in the molasses jug. Why, I didn't ask.

"Ah," he said at last, "that is just about as perfect as I can get it."

"Looks okay to me."

"Now," said Soup, "if we lure Janice into our trap, close enough to read my FREE CANDY sign, then we'll have at least half of our battle won."

I nodded. Never dispute a lunatic.

"Now," said Soup, "we best have ourselfs one more rousing chorus of our song, to be certain that we know the lyric cold."

Reaching into his pocket, Soup unfolded his musical masterpiece, and each of us inhaled a deep breath.

> "You're . . . mein . . .
> Gooten tooten high-falooten
> Pretzelsteiner gal . . ."

Nine

"Rob," said Soup, "we did it."

There we were, that afternoon, well hidden down in the tall weeds in the vacant lot behind Braunschweiger Brothers' back door.

We had the afternoon off.

No school.

Miss Kelly had a loose filling in her wisdom tooth, and had dismissed all of us at noon, in order to make an emergency visit to the dentist, Dr. DeSade. So Soup and I put our liberty to useful purpose; that being, construction.

"There," said Soup, "it's final finished."

Looking at Soup's contraption, I silently suspected that it wouldn't work. But somehow we had it assembled into one giant gizmo. Someday, I was imagining, after I'd turned old and gray *(really old,* at least thirty-five), somebody might ask me if Soup and I actual built a genuine Pretzelsteiner *spitzentootle.*

I'd proudly tell them *yes.*

Or sort of.

There we stood, among the high green weeds, staring at it. Nobody would have called it handsome. It was a large silvery hot-water tank (over the small Sterno stove) in which we had punched about twenty holes. The holes we had plugged with varying lengths of garden hose, ranging from one inch to three. At the other end of each hose was a red rubber cup that had once been part of a sink plunger. The cups, in turn, were wired to the keyboard levers of Lucky Murdock's old melodeon.

"Good thing we borrowed at least seven electrical extension cords," said Soup. "After all, cords make chords."

I winced.

"Here," he said, "be a good fellow and connect these extension cords to make one long length. Then plug in the far end to that outside outlet behind the funeral parlor."

I did it, then returned to the weeds.

"It's plugged in."

"Good," said Soup. "Now I'll attach this end to our old vacuum cleaner and find out if she blows any air."

It worked.

The vacuum sucked with almost a fanatic fury. But my friend turned it off quickly, reversed the vacuum canister, and tried it backward. Switched on, it began to blow harder than a northeaster. He attached another vacuum hose to a small pipe on the hot-water tank, which held a small amount of gurgling water. Then he approached the keyboard, now complete with all keys, including Middle C.

"Rob," he said, "I'll play, and you pray."

He pressed a white key.

SCHLOOP.

It wasn't exactly music. More like an acute case of gastric distress, produced by someone who had consumed a mixture of beans, beer, and garlic. We had invented the world's first musical note that, instead of a pitch, had an aroma.

"Soup," I said, "our music stinks. And," I added, holding my nose, "it stinks in more ways than one. It smells like The Dump."

Not to be discouraged, Soup pressed more keys, producing several disgusting chords, as well as some foul-smelling clouds. Yet, I had to admit, the so-called music did sound a lot like the original *spitzentootle* we'd heard that day from Piffle Shootensinker's truck radio. Only wetter.

Mercifully, he stopped playing. "Don't worry, Rob. It'll sound better once we light our cup of Sterno to heat the water."

Soup's dreadful music, however, seemed to linger in my ears. And in my nostrils. My pal agreed. But then a very slow grin began to spread across Soup Vinson's face, and widened into a devilish smile. Gently he nodded.

"Of course," he said softly. "Where else?"

"Where else what?" I asked. "We can't take a *spitzentootle* to the gym tomorrow night. It's too smelly. They'd never let us in the door. Besides, we don't have fifty cents each to buy a ticket to the game."

"Rob, Rob, Rob," said Soup, in a tired tone. "I have it already planned. We'll get in without a ticket. You'll see. So trust me." His face lost its smile. "It was the offensive *smell* that worried me. But I've got the answer to that too. We merely make our music in a place that smells even worse than The Dump."

"Where's that?"

Soup grinned. "The locker room."

I had to hand it to Luther Vinson. He could cover all the bases. Or most of them. It remained a mystery in my mind, however, how we'd gain admittance to the gym without a ticket. So I asked Soup how we'd pull it off.

"Simple," he said. "Because, old sport, that is where the typewriter comes in handy."

"We're going to type a ticket?"

"No. Rob, we won't even have to bother with two tickets. My plan is get into the gymnasium for *free*."

"Ah," I said, "the 'FREE CANDY.' "

"No," said Soup. "You're totally cold. Think, and you'll figure it out, Robert, old top. I wouldn't pal around with a simpleton. You have a brain. Use it. Trouble is, you've been wasting it on useless items."

"Such as?"

"Oh . . . such as *Frontiers of Norma Jean.*"

We had another problem. Our self-styled *spitzentootle* was now too heavy, especially with water sloshing around inside it, for us to carry in one piece. So we made a hurried trip to our mecca of machinery, a place to which we always turned in hours of need and stress . . . The Dump.

Here we found six wheels.

None of them were the same size, but Soup insisted that such diametric variety wouldn't really matter. As long as we could push, not carry, our *spitzentootle,* all would be well.

The six wheels were loosely attached to the belly of our horizontal hot-water tank. The tank itself was about six feet in length, yet we'd have to be able to push it through the school door. How, I wondered, would we do it? For certain, some adult of authority would prevent our entry. There we'd be, two kids without tickets, trying to crash the party with a *spitzentootle.* Our chances, as I began mentally to sum them up, appeared to be dim indeed.

"Tomorrow is Saturday," said Soup.

"Sure is."

"Well, it's our big day. Rob, tomorrow we have more construction on our agenda, but this one is, by comparison, simple."

"What is it?"

Pensively, my lifelong pal leaned on our *spitzentootle,* a faraway expression on his face. He was thinking again. Deep thoughts. Ideas that might plunge us into more trouble, like a sheep into sheep dip. Well, the sheep dip couldn't smell any worse than the notes that blooped from Soup's instrument.

"Tomorrow," said Soup, "is when we prove to the good people of Learning, our friends and neighbors, that all of the world's *sheependags* aren't residing in Pretzelstein."

"You're inventing a dog?"

Soup smiled. "No, not quite."

"But the other day, you said we'd somehow bring Adolph to Vermont, to help Piffle win the basketball game."

"True," said Soup, "in a way."

"So how do we manage all this?"

This time for certain, I was convinced, Soup Vinson had bitten off more *tootle* than he could *spitzen.* He'd claimed we now would use three plans. One, we cheer up Piffle, our homesick friend. Two, we get even with Janice, at least until she figures out her next outrage. Three, we help our home team, the Learning Groundhogs, to win Saturday evening's big basketball game.

Visions of sheepdogs, sink plungers, and jugs of molasses were now swirling through my brain, colorful images on an imaginary merry-go-round. I also could smell burning Sterno.

"Soup," I asked again, "how, in the name of good golly, are we going to use a typewriter, a jug of molasses, and a Pretzelsteiner dog? None of this makes any sense to me. What is it? Our last prank before prison? Luther Vinson's final gasp of laughing gas? And the worst part is, *you're* the sinking ship . . . and *I'm* the rat that doesn't have enough sense to jump off."

Soup laughed.

"Rob, old tiger, my closest and most trusted confederate, *now* is hardly the time to start doubting. This is it, kid. Tomorrow's the game. The Wombats from Pratt Falls are coming here to Learning, to match their basketball skills against our team. We can't let our community down. We're only boys. Yet it will be *our* efforts that will propel Learning to victory. Our men shall emerge victorious."

Soup jumped up to stand atop our *spitzentootle,* his arms raised on high, a celestial look of triumph on his face.

"Rob," he said, "we're going to win. It won't be Pratt Falls. It'll be our team. Our five." He held up five fingers on one hand. "We already know who they are, because our fifth man can't play. Shorty Smith is out with a sprained ankle. It'll be a new improved lineup. You know who."

I knew.

Merrill, Lynch, Pierce, Fenner, and Shootensinker.

Ten

Saturday came aborning.

It dawned not as most Saturdays do, stumbling into Vermont with mud on its boots, rubbing its sleep-laden eyes. This particular first Saturday of May was . . . the great day.

The game!

It would feature the Pratt Falls Wombats against our team, the Learning Groundhogs. And, as Miss Boland promised, the gym would be decorated with streamers . . . and, at the very second the game was over, all lights would be turned out and the sparklers would ignite.

It was also a time when two sterling young citizens of Learning, boys who had been raised and reared on solid

New England values and virtues, plotted to elevate the name of their town into the stratum of champions. No, it hadn't been a successful season, basketball-wise. For five players, all saddled with the nickname (or should we say diminutive) of Shorty, court victories hadn't come easily. They played as though they had breakfasted on little else but Soppies.

Things were different now.

Only four Shortys would don the Learning colors. Puce and pea green. Our fifth man, our center, would be seven feet tall; and compared to the other four, a towering Pretzelsteiner ponderosa pine.

Number 86 . . . Piffle Shootensinker.

Early, in fact presolar, on that Saturday morn of all Saturday mornings, both Soup and I were up, and girdled for battle. Needless to say, as we were the sons of farmers, both of us had our usual chores to acquit. By eight o'clock, however, Soup and I had already united in spirit and body, preparing to hurdle the obstacles that fate had shunted in our path.

First off, we suffered through one more run-through of singing Soup's abysmal song, *Mein Pretzelsteiner Gal.*

Then, fortified with the weaponry of warlocks, the brace of us set forth, toward town, intent to snatch victory from the jaws of Janice. I was silently wondering why Soup also brought a large bottle of mouthwash. Its label said GARGLE GLOW. As we hiked into town, carrying equipment, Soup had something to say.

"Rob, do you recall seeing that photograph that Piffle showed us, the one of his shaggy *sheependag*?"

"Sure, I remember Adolph."

"Did he remind you of anybody?"

I nodded. "But I can't remember who."

Soup grinned. "Tonight, you will."

"Where are we headed, Soup?"

Using a hammer, Soup pointed straight ahead. I looked where he was pointing. It was the sheepshearing shed.

"Soup," I asked as we walked, "as to what we're intending to do . . . is it related to sheep?" It was a dumb question, and I knew it. Yet, since I was currently harboring such a multitude of stupidity, one question, more or less, seemed to be of little consequence.

"Sort of," came Soup's clarifying response.

"Oh, I see."

Actually, I didn't. Nor did I understand the importance of my having to spend a penny, to purchase three-for-a-cent molasses kisses, the ones wrapped in gray tissue paper, twisted at both ends. And I couldn't fathom the jug of molasses or the sign . . . FREE CANDY . . . that Soup was carrying.

We arrived at the shearing shed.

"Here we are," Soup said.

"Good."

"And right here," Soup added, "is where we build what will someday be described, in the athletic history of Learning, as The Molasses Miracle."

"Right here?"

He nodded. "Correct. First, we shall more or less construct a sort of cage."

This we did. It wasn't difficult, because we used a wool-baling box, one that was five feet tall, five feet wide, and five feet across. The wooden box was composed of slats, boards that were three or four inches wide.

"Perfect," said Soup.

I shrugged. "Perfect for what?"

"You'll see."

Having the sense not to inquire, I assisted Soup in the simple construction of a trapdoor. It was attached to the eye-screw of an upside-down jug, full of molasses. One yank of that cork, Soup explained, would drench any unfortunate inhabitant of the wool box. He'd be anointed with the stickiest of substances. Molasses. A year ago, helping Papa handle a silo chore, I'd frosted myself with molasses, by accident.

It stuck all over me.

Like glue.

We suspended the fake baling box in the mouth of a barn shaft, a place where wool fell into a retaining bin, ready to be shipped. Below was a deep pile of raw wool. Outside our trap we nailed Soup's hand-painted sign.

FREE CANDY

"Now," said Soup, "we are ready."

Ready, I was wondering, for what? It was a mite confusing, imagining how a basketball game could be won by wool. Not to mention a jug of molasses. The sign that read FREE CANDY was beyond comprehension.

Speaking of signs, it was at that precise moment when my pal decided to show me his other sign. I'd thought he'd only brought one. Wrong. His second sign read as follows:

DANGER

HIGH VOLTAGE

DO NOT TOUCH

"Soup, what's the danger sign for?"

"It's for tonight," he said.

He was busy making certain that the jugful of molasses was positioned exactly in the middle of the cage's roof. Again he checked his lanyard of twine, one end of which would dislodge the cork from the jug.

"As the trapdoor opens," Soup was now explaining, "the twine pulls tight, and it pops out the cork. And," he said, beaming, "the sticky molasses flows like wine."

"Okay," I said, "as long as I don't get any molasses on either me or my clothes."

"Ah," said Soup, "speaking of molasses, do you still have your penny?"

Reaching into my trouser pocket, I produced it with a fond gesture of farewell.

"Your job," Soup told me, "is to go and spend it, over at Jubert's Candy Store. But make sure you purchase molasses kisses."

"Right," I said, "three for a cent."

I left, bought the candy, and returned to where Soup stood, outside the shearing shed, admiring his work. He'd moved a short ladder closer to our cage box, our trap. Yet the sign, FREE CANDY, couldn't be clearly seen, a fact I quickly pointed out to my pal.

"Don't worry about that," Soup said. "Tonight, just before the basketball game, somebody will see it."

"Who?"

"Somebody who just might play an important part in Learning's victory over Pratt Falls."

As we left the shearing barn, heading toward the vacant lot where our *spitzentootle* lay waiting in the weeds, I asked Soup if he really thought that our team had a chance to win tonight.

"Yup," said Soup, flashing me a thumbs-up gesture in absolute confidence. "A slim chance."

"But our players haven't won a game all season. Not even one."

"Yet," said Soup, "whenever Learning can defeat Pratt Falls, most folks here in town usual smile, and claim we had a winner of a winter."

Our *spitzentootle* was there, well hidden in the high weedy greenery of the vacant lot. The six wheels didn't appear to be overly sturdy. Yet I hoped they would prove stout enough to roll our musical instrument as far as the high school gym.

Soup snapped his fingers.

"We forgot something."

"What?"

"The typewriter."

We hurried to The Dump, a handy haven where a devout searcher could generally locate anything, found a busted typewriter that sort-of worked, and then spotted a small scrap of white paper. Placing the rusty old typewriter atop a rotting barrel, Soup sat on a dirty crate, loosened his fingers, and then inserted our paper beneath the roller.

"Here goes," said Soup. Then he looked up at me, after pecking out a few letters. "Rob," he asked, "how do you spell Braunschweiger?"

With difficulty, I spelled it.

"It doesn't look right to me," said Soup. "Are you certain Braunschweiger has two *J*'s in it? Maybe I should just say Boris and Lavoris."

He completed the message while I watched from over his shoulder.

"There," he said. "It's all done. Now we'll scoot over yonder to the high school and pin this note to the door, where Mr. McGillicuddy will see it. And tonight, as I see it, if you don't mind getting a tiny little dab of molasses on your hair, it's the only way that two swell guys can sneak into the basketball game."

"Without a ticket?" I asked.

Soup looked at me and smiled.

"Free," he said. "Free as candy."

Eleven

We ran.

It was Saturday evening, at last. Our chores were done, supper eaten, so Soup and I headed for town.

"Well," said Soup as we arrived at the vacant lot and the tall weeds, "at least our *spitzentootle* is still here."

"All we do now," I said hopefully, "is go to the basketball game, get in free, and enjoy watching our friend Piffle play."

"Not quite," said Soup.

The way he said it lowered my blood temperature by a good twenty degrees. Trouble is a chilling sensation.

"First," said Soup, "we each have a duty to perform. I'll

push our *spitzentootle* and coveralls in the direction of the shearing shed, while you go and fetch Janice Riker."

I swallowed. This isn't easily done when one's throat already feels as if it's being throttled. Janice was sometimes known, at school, as The Vermont Strangler.

"Janice?"

"Right. She's part of my master plan. You recall . . . one of our three plans."

Soup began to push the *spitzentootle* out of the weeds and across the open area of the vacant lot.

"Hold it," I said. "Why don't I push this thing, and *you* go after Janice?"

Soup sighed. "Because," he explained, "you're the one who has the molasses candy. That's only fair. After all, it was your penny."

"How," I asked Soup, "do I get Janice? And once I locate her, what do I do with her?"

"Simple," said Soup. "You bring her to the shearing shed. You know, where our trap is. When you get to Janice's house, she'll probably be there. Wherever you hear an animal scream, or a kid yelping in pain, you'll find Janice. Then you run by her and yell 'Free candy,' good and loud. Show her that you already are eating some. Drop a molasses kiss. A fish has to nibble the worm. Then you'll lead her to where I'll be waiting at the shearing barn. There's an electrical outlet there, so I can use the *spitzentootle.* Even with cold water."

"Okay," I sighed. "But if I die, please find a way to tell me who won tonight's big game."

"It's a deal," said Soup.

Believe it or not, I actual went in search of Janice, yelling "Free candy!" She heard, saw, and took after me like a hungry cat behind a slow mouse. I led her toward our trap, dropping a molasses kiss. Janice picked it up, and, without removing its paper wrapper, swallowed it whole. Never had I seen Janice bother to chew. Except on another kid's ear.

Soup, meanwhile, was playing (or attempting to play) a Pretzelsteiner polka on his *spitzentootle.* Out of breath, I pointed, and Janice looked at our sign.

FREE CANDY

"Janice," I hollered at her from a safe distance of fifty yards, "you can't go up that ladder. That's all *my* candy up there. I discovered it first. So keep away."

What kid, I silently asked myself, could resist free candy? Looking at Janice, it seemed as if she was already smelling the jug of molasses. Yet she didn't attempt to climb the ladder.

PLOOP burped the *spitzentootle.*

"What's that creepy noise?" Janice asked.

"Oh," I said, "that's . . . uh . . . that's the candy-making machine. It makes molasses kisses. But don't go up there, Janice. All that *free candy* is mine."

Would it work?

I watched Janice Riker reading Soup's sign once again, a puzzled look on her face. "Free candy," Janice was growling. "Nobody gives candy away for free."

My heart sank. Janice wasn't about to take the bait. So, right then, I had to act quickly.

"Right," I said. "There's no candy up there." As I said it, I pulled my third (and last) molasses kiss from my pocket, unwrapped it, and popped it into my mouth.

"Liar," snarled Janice. "There's candy up there in that box. *Free* candy. And I'm going up there and take it all myself."

"Oh, Janice, please don't." It was a phrase I'd used many a torturous time over the years. Yet tonight, it was a rapturous retort.

Up the ladder she charged, her chunky legs churning like the pistons on an eighteen wheeler. But then, reaching the top ladder rung, she stopped cold. Janice wasn't going to fall for it. It was no dice. Holding my breath, I watched her sniff around like a suspicious hound dog. She even stopped to scratch a flea. And then, inch by inch, Janice entered our cage. Once she was inside our prepared wool box, underneath the upside-down jug of molasses, the trapdoor gave way. Out popped the cork! A gallon of sticky brown molasses cascaded on Janice's head. Down she tumbled, through the trapdoor, landing safely in the deep pile of freshly cut wool below, in the wool bin.

All I heard, as Janice Riker disappeared down into the

thick wool, was one sheepish word. More of a naughty word than it was sheepish. It certainly wasn't *baa*.

Well, I thought, that would be the last we'd see of Janice Riker this evening.

"Come on," said Soup, who suddenly appeared around the corner of the barn. He didn't look at all like the Soup Vinson I knew, as he was wearing a pair of white coveralls. Turning around once, he displayed the name that was printed on the back.

BORIS

"Hurry," said Soup. "The game's about to start, and we may run into difficulty without a ticket. But it's a good thing we put the typewritten note on the entrance door."

Smelling trouble, I nonetheless continued to follow Soup's mysterious directions. When he tossed me the other pair of white coveralls, I jumped into them. We put molasses (as there was plenty around) on our hair, and then added some fuzzy wool.

To my surprise, Soup began to look a lot like Boris Braunschweiger. And I, like Lavoris, his twin brother.

Soup's plan was taking form. But why he was draining all of the water from the tank was certainly a mystery to me. He replaced it with Gargle Glow (the mouthwash of Movie Stars).

"Let's go," he told me. "Push."

The two of us pushed our *spitzentootle* about as rapidly

as possible, considering its six wheels of varying size. The instrument had a strange gait, a forward-rolling motion somewhere between lame and halt. Arriving at the gymnasium door, we were stopped by the elderly gentleman who was taking tickets.

"Let *me* do the talking," Soup whispered, so I allowed him to handle our conversation. Soup pointed at the note that we had earlier pinned to the door.

> Mr. McGillicuddy:
> Please let Boris and Lavoris inside to repair the plumbing and the janitor's closet. They will bring a large tool.
>
> Miss Boland

The man who was taking tickets, luckily for Soup and me, was old Mr. McGillicuddy, nearing eighty in years, hard-of-hearing and dim of sight. For many a decade, he had performed odd jobs around the high school.

"Gotta have a ticket," he cackled.

Soup smiled broadly, and said, *"Mein hooperdunken izt no-goot stinken midout der spitzentootle und sheependag."* He pointed at me, then himself, and finally at the *spitzentootle*. Then, turning me around, he showed the LAVORIS on my coveralls to Mr. McGillicuddy. As he pointed at the "Lavoris" in the typewritten note, the old gent squinted at it.

"Ah," said Mr. McGillicuddy with a comprehending

nod, "you're the Spanish orchestra from Hodge Corners.
Come on in."

We entered.

Free!

Once inside, Soup and I noticed the new construction
above and beyond the gymnasium. There were ramps,
pipes, lumber, and several piles of cement bags. Quickly
we parked our *spitzentootle* in the hall outside the visiting
team's locker room, and placed Soup's sign on it.

> DANGER
>
> HIGH VOLTAGE
>
> DO NOT TOUCH

Right then, as we stood in the hall, a sudden cheer rose
from all partisan throats, coming from the gym.

"Let's go watch," said Soup, "as soon as I light a match
to the Sterno to heat the mouthwash in our tank. Our
music will smell better."

"Hurry," I said. "The game's about to start."

In we crept. The gymnasium was lavishly festooned
with colored crepe streamers, no doubt a result of Miss
Boland's fidelity to festivity. Out on the basketball court,
Coach Brutus Beefjerky, our local football coach (who
tried to coach a few non-school sports as well) had started
to give his final instructions to our Learning five. I could
identify our Groundhogs and their numbers. Piffle, as a
last-minute substitute for Smith, wore one of the old uni-

forms . . . helmet, knickers, and high-laced boots. So his number was somewhat out of sequence with those of his four teammates:

1	Shorty Merrill	guard
2	Shorty Lynch	guard
3	Shorty Pierce	forward
4	Shorty Fenner	forward
86	Piffle Shootensinker	center

Another cheer roared through the crowd, this one mild by comparison, as the visiting team, the Pratt Falls Wombats, raced out of their locker room and onto the court. Their numbers, names, and positions were announced by the referee:

1	Stretch Murphy	guard
2	Stretch Millerton	guard
3	Stretch Marx	center
4	Stretch Millerton	forward
5	Stretch Murphy	forward

"Notice," said Soup, "that four out of five Pratt Falls Wombats are either Millertons or Murphys. A pity," he said slyly, "that both of those families share a seasonal disorder."

The ball was tossed into the air, at center court, by the referee, wearing his official striped pajama top.

The game was on!

But it wasn't any picnic for our Learning Groundhogs, in uniforms of puce and pea green. The seconds ticked by. The score mounted. At the halftime buzzer, I couldn't bear to look at the scoreboard. Yet I did.

| Pratt Falls | 2 |
| Learning | 0 |

Twelve

We stood up.

So did everyone else. Because at halftime, during any Vermont basketball game, this intermission is known as the Seventh Inning Stretch, a custom that probable originated in Pratt Falls.

Stretches usual do.

"Unless we act during the second half, Pratt Falls," quipped Soup, "is rebound to win."

Coach Beefjerky was jittery too. I noticed that during much of the first half he had helpfully yelled, "Block that kick."

Kids were running around the gym, making noise. Eddy Tacker jumped up and yanked several of the colored crepe paper streamers. They now hung in listless defeat. Three streamers, however, fell across the backboard of one of the baskets, in tatters.

Now, out on the court, the halftime show was in full swing. Our only cheerleader, Miss Kimberly Knocknee, was vainly trying to inspire the hometowners with a rousing (but nutty) cheer:

> Walnut, almond,
> Filbert, pecan.
> Who can win it?
> *We* can. *We* can!

Nobody cheered. Perhaps the spectators realized that the second half, as so many sportscasters enjoy saying, might be a grim replica of the first. A good many of the fans had forsaken their seats to visit the rest rooms, or to buy hot dogs and soda pop at the refreshment counter.

I spotted Miss Boland.

She was standing near a large carton, the label of which read: DIXIE FIREWORKS COMPANY. Our nurse was selecting a few boxes of sparklers for the end-of-the-game celebration . . . win or lose.

"Rob," said Soup, as he eyed the dismal figures that Mr.

McGillicuddy had hung on the scoreboard, "it's time we made our move."

"Right," I said.

We moved.

Seeing as Soup and I didn't look at all as we usually appeared, as Luther Vinson and Robert Peck, we could go anywhere in the school. Disguised as Boris and Lavoris, the Braunschweiger twins, we were (to the public's disinterested eye) merely two elderly repairmen doing whatever it was that plumbers and janitors do.

We went to our *spitzentootle.*

Placing his hand on the large silvery hot-water tank, Soup looked at me, and then smiled.

"Good," he said. "The mouthwash is heated. But maybe we'll sound better if we let it get a few degrees hotter. Is the flame in the Sterno can still burning?"

I looked underneath the tank.

"Yup. Still burning."

"Well," said Soup, "our next step is to push our secret weapon here, our *spitzentootle,* into the locker room."

I looked up the hall.

"We can't. Not right now."

"Why not?" Soup asked me.

"Because the team is in there, no doubt listening to a rousing halftime speech by Coach Beefjerky on the possible joys of victory."

For once, I was right.

Just then, the locker room door busted open and out poured our town basketball team in their puce and pea-green uniforms, led by Coach Beefjerky himself, the old football coach.

"Okay, you guys," he hollered back over his shoulder, "let's get back on that field and make a few tackles."

"Now," said Soup, "into the locker room we go. Come on, Rob . . . *push.*"

We pushed.

Into the locker room we sped, *spitzentootle* and all, inhaling an odor that would make sheep dip seem like an expensive perfume, such as Evening in Paris, or even Morning in Rutland.

Outside, the second half began.

Merrill, Lynch, Pierce, Fenner, and Shootensinker all were suddenly playing their hearts out for dear old Learning. Yet first-half momentum refused to reverse. They tried off-tackle, an end run, even a forward pass . . . but nothing seemed to click. Piffle carried the ball but couldn't make yardage. His shots all drifted astray. One shot merely knocked more streamers loose. Unlike the ball, the long crepe papers fell into the netting of the basket.

"Quick," said Soup, "find a wall socket, so we can plug in our *spitzentootle* and play."

I found one.

In went our extension cord plug.

"Try it," I told Soup.

He tried it. No sound.

"It must be dead," he said. "Rob, find another outlet."

I looked around. "There aren't any."

"Well," said Soup, "we sure as heck can't stay and play our music in here."

"Where'll we go?"

Soup darted out the door and then returned in less than two minutes. "I've got it," he said, smiling. "Remember all that construction we saw? We'll push our machine up that long ramp."

"Where to?"

"Up to the band balcony that overlooks the gym. As this isn't a high school game, their band isn't here. And there's an electrical outlet up there. I just checked."

"Let's go," I said.

Out into the gym we went, pushing our *spitzentootle*, staying clear of the basketball court, using the aisle behind the bleacher seats. Up the ramp we went. The ramp was a slanted incline, made up of a series of many plywood planks. Each piece was four feet by eight feet.

It was a long push.

But we finally made it to the gym balcony, and the two of us stopped for breath.

Right then, I heard a rumble.

"What was that?" I asked.

"It's raining outside," said Soup. "What we just heard was thunder. We may be getting Vermont's first thunderstorm of the summer."

Again, the thunder sounded.

Much louder.

"Okay," said Soup. "Over there is the electrical socket. Plug 'er in and keep your fingers crossed that we've got some juice."

I plugged. Soup pressed a key.

BLORPTZ.

"Hooray," said Soup, "it final works."

"How's it sound?"

"Perfect," he said. "I can't wait for Piffle to hear his beloved Pretzelsteiner music. Rob, are you ready to sing?"

I sighed. "Ready."

As Soup's fingers flew over the keyboard, for an instrumental introduction, I cleared the frog from my throat (possibly a toad) and prepared to sing the most important solo of my life . . . *Mein Pretzelsteiner Gal:*

> You're . . . mein . . .
> Gooten, tooten, high-falooten
> Pretzelsteiner gal. You can
> Puckerup und kissen me insane.

I kin
Baken you a strudel. Kit
Kaboodle und a noodle, so itz
Schmelling like a poodle in der rain.

Pretzelsteiner baby, you kin
Stoppit saying "maybe." Say a
"Jah" and maken me a schmiling pal.

You're . . . mein . . .
Schnitzel, you're mein wiener. You're mein
Frankfurters und beaner. You're mein
Sour krauten Pretzelsteiner
Gal.

It worked!

Down on the court, Piffle Shootensinker was now playing every bit as well as our former star, Shorty Smith, and maybe even a point or two better. Stealing the ball from one of the Pratt Falls Wombats, he dribbled halfway down the court, cocked his long arm, and fired a forty-foot jumper. Over the heads of Stretch Murphy and Stretch Millerton.

Whoosh!

The score was tied. Dead even.

Pratt Falls	2
Learning	2

But then the buzzer sounded, ending the third quarter of this high-scoring Vermont basketball classic. What would the fourth and final quarter bring? Victory for our Groundhogs? Or the dismal dungeon of defeat? Crepe streamers sagged sadly into one of the baskets.

The fourth quarter started.

Yet neither team seemed able to score. A brilliant attempt by Shorty Merrill was easily blocked by Stretch Murphy. To make matters worse, something went amuck with our *spitzentootle*. It gushed a few isolated sounds . . . a PLOOP here, or a PLOP there . . . yet it somehow refused to gargle another rousing chorus of *Mein Pretzelsteiner Gal.*

But then . . .

The first foul of the game. The ref's whistle shrieked at the infraction, and Stretch Marx toed the foul line. After nervously bouncing the ball seventy-three times, sometimes under one leg and then behind the other, reciting a cute little verse while bouncing . . . "Strawberry shortcake, huckleberry pie, I love you and you love I" . . . Stretch arched his shot.

Unluckily for us, it sank. Moans escaped local lips. In agony I gazed at the gymnasium scoreboard, reading the tormenting truth:

Pratt Falls	3
Learning	2

Seconds ticked by. Precious seconds. The fourth quarter sped along its inevitable tour of time, seemingly intent upon a futile finale. But then our hopes brightened. Soup discovered that some of his head wool had lodged itself between the keys of his keyboard. Now free, the *spitzentootle* was once again operative.

Soup played.

I sang.

Perhaps, as fate would have it, this would be my final chorus of *Mein Pretzelsteiner Gal*; and, seeing as she was in the crowd, my final opportunity to impress Norma Jean Bissell with my heartfelt ballad of bliss.

So, heedless to say, I sang with every tonsil within me, each note gussied to a prawltriller, and each syllable, a mordent. Yet the roar of the crowd somehow seemed to stifle even my highest tenor (or adolescent alto) shrieks. On one occasion, my vocal chords even neared the celestial pitch of High C. I began to hit notes in the upper registers that would have inspired a choir of mosquitoes. Or head lice.

No one heard.

The gymnasium fans were too vocal to need my piccolodic pleas. Several were snoring.

I looked at the scoreboard clock.

Only one minute remained.

Sixty precious seconds.

Then fifty-nine.

Fifty-eight.

"Rob," hollered Soup, "we gotta do something, because our Groundhogs are going to lose."

"But what?" I answered him.

Soup gazed Heavenward. "What we need," he said, "is some sort of a miracle. Please, send us an *angel.*"

The crowd stilled.

As though Soup's imploring had been heard, Upstairs, and answered . . . all eyes ceased following the basketball game. Everybody was looking at the gymnasium door. Someone had arrived. An angel from Heaven? No. It was a dog. And better yet, not just any dog, because this appeared to be a genuine *sheependag* . . . from Pretzelstein.

It, I could have sworn, was Adolph.

In it came, on its hind legs, looking shaggy and woolly, much like the photograph that Piffle Shootensinker had shown us. Yet this, I abruptly realized was no average dog. Why? Because this *sheependag* could talk.

"I'll kill 'em," the dog was snarling. "And when I catch up to Rob and Soup, I'm gonna punch out their lights."

"No," I said.

"Yes," said Soup, with a smile. "It isn't a *sheependag.* Don't let all that stuck-on wool fool you. It's Janice."

My brain was reckoning, remembering, recalling how the photo of a sheepdog that Piffle showed us reminded me of something, or of someone, I knew. It was like Lavoris and Boris Braunschweiger. Adolph, the Pretzelsteiner *sheependag,* and Janice Riker were practically twins.

"Grrrr," growled Janice.

I cringed.

Thirteen

"Adolph," hollered Piff.

I looked at the scoreboard clock, hoping that Piffle could improve, inspired by his dog.

Only twenty seconds left to play. There was, I was surmising, little chance for a victory for our home team, the Learning Groundhogs. This would be a sad moment for our colors, the puce and pea green.

But then, sensing that wafts of change now blew in the wind, the gymnasium audience seemed to fantasize that perhaps we could win. Glum expressions were replaced by hope. Eyebrows lifted. Aspiration soared, as though awing. Then, it happened. Someone in the crowd, some unknown sporting fan whose name shall never grace the pages of *Great Sporting Moments,* began to chant. Perhaps no one heard him, or her, not at first. Yet a second voice chimed in. And a third.

"We want a touchdown."

No rhyme nor reason could ever dare to explain why, or how, yet this inappropriate chant gradually became contagious, infecting every throat like a strep virus. Larynx after larynx, trachea upon trachea took up the call, chanting in rapturous unison:

"We wanna touchdown."

Ten seconds to play.

Nine seconds.

Eight.

In the bleachers, money began to exchange hands. Not paltry wagers. These were big-timers and high rollers, laying odds, as the currency involved skyrocketed beyond a quarter. Some local hotshot, shucking away all Vermont restraint and fiduciary prudence, awed those around him by risking fifty cents.

Seven seconds.

Six.

The moment came. As Janice went roaring and racing around the court, in search of Soup Vinson and Rob Peck to tear us asunder, her errant wool dust began adversely to affect four of the five Pratt Falls players. Both the Murphys and the Millertons began to sneeze and wheeze.

"Sheepensneezer," said Soup. "Rob, remember what we both read at the Learning Free Library, about Pretzelstein?"

"What is it?"

"That some people, even over in faraway Pretzelstein, are allergic to wool." He pointed at the court. "It's working. Four out of five Pratt Falls players are sneezing their heads off."

I looked.

Soup was right.

Murphy, Murphy, Millerton, and Millerton were sneezing to beat the band. For sure, Janice Riker, and all her molasses-stuck wool, had brought the *sheepensneezer* curse to the opposing team. Marx, their fifth player, seemed none too healthy. Then, with the Pratt Falls players in a state of indispose, Shorty Merrill stole the ball . . . and passed. Merrill to Lynch to Pierce to Fenner to Shootensinker.

"Punt," yelled Coach Beefjerky.

"Shoot," hollered all the rest of us to Piffle.

Only four seconds to play, and old Mr. McGillicuddy stood ready, poised at the light switch.

Three seconds.

Two.

The scoreboard numbers, also managed by Mr. McGillicuddy, remained unchanged:

Pratt Falls   3
Learning   2

One second left. But in that one wink of time, Piffle, with *hooperdunken* heritage surging through his veins, aroma of wool, a vision of his beloved *sheependag* named Adolph, plus the pungent lingerings of *Mein Pretzelsteiner Gal* still lodged in both nostrils like some alien allergy, hooked the basketball upward.

And hoopward.

But the final buzzer sounded.

No matter. Piffle's hook shot was en route, arching majestically toward our basket, and to victory. If it went in, we'd win.

But the outcome of sporting events is never quite that simple. How easy it would be, to report how the Learning Groundhogs had won the game. Yet, in all tribute to honesty, I cannot. Why? Because of Miss Boland's explicit instructions to Mr. McGillicuddy, the ticket taker. He of almost countless years and waxing faculties. Miss Boland, our county nurse, had told him to flick off the gymnasium lights at the precise split second the final buzzer buzzed.

This he did.

All we now saw were sparklers, which, one by one, burned themselves out. We were all momentarily blinded.

The result?

Well, as the lights went out, plunging all of us into sparkling darkness, nobody could say for sure and certain whether Piffle Shootensinker's final shot had entered the basket. Or not. Nary a living soul could attest, for the record, which team had indeed won the game. All sparkler-dazzled eyes blinked in confusion.

In unison, a groan escaped every mouth in the gymnasium. For there we final were, immersed in blackness, wondering whether or not Number 86, of the puce and pea green, had dunked his determining shot.

"Hey," said Soup, "I can't see."

"Neither," I said, "can I."

"Did Piffle's shot go in?"

"Who knows? Nobody in this gymnasium. Maybe the entire game will be protested, and have to be replayed . . . in July."

All was quiet. But then I heard a hollow voice, plaintive words coming from the man who, in his prime, had played years of football without a helmet, Coach Beefjerky:

> "Hit 'em again. Hit 'em again.
> Harder. Harder."

Perhaps the coach didn't yet realize that the game was over. He was entirely in darkness. So were we all. Nobody could see a thing. Pitch-black.

"I'll *get* them two," Janice snorted.

But then the lights went on again, and everyone

blinked at everybody else. Only one question was asked. *Who won the game?* Nobody knew. Did our towering center, Piffle, sink his final shot? No one could answer. Did the ball go through the hoop, or did it miss?

Where, I wondered, *is* the ball? Looking around, I couldn't see it anywhere. Had a thief stolen the basketball? None of the Pratt Falls Wombats had it. Neither did the Learning Groundhogs. Soup noticed it too.

"Where's the ball?" he asked.

Then it happened.

We were all in our seats, too stupefied to move a muscle. Yet into the gym shuffled old Mr. McGillicuddy, carrying a broom, a mop, and a tall stepladder. Calmly, he set down the mop and broom, leaning them against a wall. Everybody watched him, transfixed, as he placidly went about his usual business of tidying up the gym following a game, as he had done for so many years.

Setting up the ladder beneath one of the backboards, the old gentleman slowly climbed it. One step, a second step, a third. At the top step he paused, reached upward, and removed the ball from the basket. For there it was, stuck inside the netting, because of some crepe streamers in there too.

We couldn't breathe.

Nobody moved.

Mr. McGillicuddy climbed down, walked calmly to the scoreboard, and made a casual correction of the numerals.

Pratt Falls	3
Learning	4

"Holy cow," Soup was screaming. "We won!"

"Hooray," I was hollering.

PA-BLOOP went the *spitzentootle,* as if in some private celebration of its own.

The gymnasium crowd, Vermonters all, refused to go crazy. It was as if they had all expected Learning to win, even after the final buzzer. Generations of restraint, however, final gave way. Somebody quietly mumbled, "Pay up."

A dime reluctantly exchanged hands.

Fourteen

Ka-booommm.

It happened all at once.

A bolt of lightning hit the school. And then, a split second later, came the loudest explosion of thunder that I had ever heard. My teeth hurt.

I felt the bones in my toes crackle.

"Wow," said Soup.

The lights in the gym went out again. Yet we were not without light. Why not? Because our *spitzentootle* was still plugged in. The sudden electrical surge seemed to cause our music machine to come instantly alive. Like a rearing horse, the *spitzentootle* sprang suddenly upward, showering Soup and me with hundreds of sparks. Then it lit up like a large lamp. Ghostlike, it glowed in the dark.

And it played.

By itself.

BLORP. KAPOOT. PZTFX. TOOTLESPITZ.

It wasn't really genuine music.

More like a war. Or a factory.

Forward it bolted.

"Grab it," Soup yelled. "We can't let it roll down the ramp. It'll go too close to the bleachers."

Electricity has always scared me skinny. I won't even touch a dead battery. But now, despite my fear, there I really was. I'd jumped up on top of the *spitzentootle,* as had Soup, and was holding on, trying to rein it back under control.

GLUPZTX. KROOPZ. BXT.

The *spitzentootle* had a mind, however, of its own. Or so it seemed. Worse yet, the noises all had smells. None of them were fragrant, despite occasional fumes of Gargle Glow.

Down the ramp it charged, *charged* with enough electrical power to illuminate every light bulb in Vermont, activate all the washers and dryers of New Hampshire, and to short-circuit half of the toasters in Maine and Massachusetts.

Did it roll smoothly?

Not quite. Not on six wheels, none of which matched the other five in diameter. It didn't roll. It bucked.

"Soup," I yelped, "what'll we do?"

His answer came in one inspired word.

"Pray."

Down the plywood ramp we rambled, gaining speed, spitting sparks to the left and to the right, and burping the mouthwash of Movie Stars. Ahead, in total darkness, I began to see the startled openmouthed faces of Learning sports fans. Their eyes were widening in horror, too transfixed even to scream.

Who could blame them?

Few are the folks who can stand their ground when caught directly in the path of a runaway *spitzentootle*. Vermont is a far piece away from Pretzelstein. As far as I knew, only three people in the town of Learning had ever seen a musical monster such as ours. It emitted smoke, sparks, noise, and the worst smell this side of a beauty parlor. Plus the undeniable fact that it was being ridden by two small boys.

Yet all the news wasn't bad.

Some was good.

We were headed point-blank at Janice Riker.

"It's gonna hit that dog," somebody said.

"I hope so," said someone else, "because that there confounded mutt just came up . . . and would you believe it . . . kicked me in the shin."

"Soup," I said, "when you built this tomfool thing, you forgot to add something."

"What?"

"A brake."

Forward we bolted, headlong down the ramp, toward a gymnasium of utter darkness. And worse . . . right toward Janice. She was facing us, fangs bared, claws up and ready to strike, her chunky body prepared to destroy even an onrushing truck. But a renegade *spitzentootle* turned out to be beyond even Janice Riker's coping.

Wham.

Into old Janice we crashed.

It felt as though we'd hit a brick wall.

Or, perhaps, an Army tank.

At the very split second of impact, I heard Janice's comment. One word. A real cusser. Nothing fancy. Her word was just an old favorite. A genuine zinger. It was a word that Miss Kelly, my mother, and Soup's mother had warned us *never* to use.

It didn't actual make me angry.

But, strangely enough, Janice Riker's swearword seemed to enrage our *spitzentootle*. It went crazy. Berserk. Nuts. As if every bolt and volt of celestial electricity had spurred it into some sort of fanatic frenzy. Not many people, and certainly none in Vermont, had ever confronted a mad *spitzentootle*.

Through the crowd it plowed, mowing people down as if they were bowling pins.

Ahead of me, I saw the good citizens of Learning diving this way, and that, in an effort to avoid our insane instrument.

Worst of all, Janice landed.

Not in the crowd.

Janice Riker, following our crash, landed on top of the speeding *spitzentootle*, exactly between Soup and me. Would she recognize us? Nobody else had. To everyone in the LHS gymnasium, Soup and I were Boris and Lavoris, janitor and plumber.

"Hey," I heard Janice growl, "any of youse old gents seen a couple of yellow-belly boys?"

I didn't answer.

Soup did. *"Mein hooperdunken izt no gooten stinken und mein sheepen got der sheepensneezer."*

"Forget it," said Janice. "I don't speak South American."

Meanwhile, the *spitzentootle* had sideswiped a corner of one of the bleachers, and went headlong through the refreshment stand. On my upper lip, I tasted mustard. And catsup. But there was no slowing down of our electrical steed. Forward it charged.

The gym was still without lights.

Except for our sparks.

Ahead, I saw something.

But I didn't want to believe what I saw.

Nevertheless, it was true.

The closer we came, the more convinced I was of a greater impending disaster, one that just couldn't be allowed to happen, yet was about to take place.

"Yikes," I said.

Soup saw it too. "Holy cow."

If old Janice saw it, she wasn't bright enough to realize the full repercussions of the tragedy about to befall us all.

"What's that box?" Janice asked.

I didn't answer her. There was no way that I'd betray my identity. Not when old Janice Riker and I were riding the same *spitzentootle*.

Nonetheless, I stared at the box.

There it sat, harmless enough, dead ahead and directly in our path. The electrical sparks that scattered from our mindless machine were enough to light up the letters. The name grew larger . . . and larger . . .

DIXIE FIREWORKS COMPANY.

"No," I whispered. "I mean *nein*."

"Yes," Soup responded. *"Jah."*

"Hey," said Janice, "youse two funny old guys ain't sounding like no Boris and Lavoris."

She was starting to understand. But for her, and us, it came a second or so too late. Something else was taking over. A box. One with a label that read: DIXIE FIREWORKS COMPANY.

I knew what the box held.

In school, sometime last Monday, our county nurse had explained it all. Miss Boland, who somehow was always in charge of just about everything in town, had told our entire class about it. All of the community's Fourth of July fireworks had arrived, a few weeks early. They were safely housed in a carton, at the high school, where nothing or nobody could possible ignite them.

"Don't worry," Soup was yelling.

"Why not?"

"Because," he explained, "even if we bang into the box, we can't ignite those fireworks without flame."

"Good," I said.

That was when I felt something.

Somebody very mean.

It was Janice.

"Hey," she snarled, "youse guys ain't the Braunschweiger brothers. I know who youse guys are. You're . . ."

Luckily (or perhaps *unluckily* if you reconsider the hapless ending of a local gentleman by the name of Lucky Murdock) old Janice was never allowed to complete her final remark.

Why not?

Because my pal Soup had forgotten one small, yet very pivotal, fact.

There was flame.

Where?

Beneath us.

Underneath the hot-water tank.

It was the reason our *spitzentootle* mouthwash was hot. We should have known. Sterno. The burning Sterno.

Crash.

Into the carton of Dixie Fireworks we rammed. Very

hard. Sterno and all. A second passed. Two seconds. Three. *KAAAA-BOOOOOOOOMMM.*

In fact, it was May.

All over the world, the merry month of May.

Not in Learning. Oh no. In the modest little hamlet of Learning, Vermont . . . it was another month . . . another day.

It was suddenly July 4.

Several weeks early.

In the gymnasium, there was no electricity. But no matter, there was still a lot of light. All of it was explosions. Large firecrackers. Roman candles. Skyrockets in at least thirteen varying colors.

Outdoors, on a Fourth of July evening, the bombs manage to make noise aplenty. But in the confines of a high school gym, it was nothing short of a world war. The end of everything. One gigantic explosion, followed by another, and another, that split eardrums and scorched hair.

Someone spoke.

"I dropped my dime," he said.

"That's okay," said his neighbor. "At least we beat Pratt Falls."

"Well, I'll say this for that crazy Boland woman. She sure knows how to stage a victory celebration."

Slowly the explosions began to subside.

Quiet was restored.

The gymnasium lights flickered and came back on.

"Wow," said Soup, "I sure learned my lesson. Never again will I ever attempt to construct a *spitzentootle.*"

Janice tapped him on the shoulder.

"Guess what?" she asked Soup. "Now that the lights are *on*, Luther, I'm going to put yours *out.*"

Just then, along came Piffle.

He lifted Soup high in the air, with one hand. Then he lifted me with the other. We were saved.

"Hooperdunken," he said, *"izt gooten."*

It's great to have a seven-foot pal.

Fifteen

That night, I dreamed again.

Perhaps, because of so many bizarre activities on that Saturday evening, my night's fantasy was the best ever. I was seven feet tall and a star basketballer.

Stretch Peck.

In my dream, I launched a seventy-foot hooker that scored the winning basket into, of all things, Soup's hoop. My teammates were Miss Kelly, Mr. McGillicuddy, Miss Boland, my mother, Soup, and both Boris and Lavoris, who played in coveralls.

We all played against Piffle.

The referee was Baron Wolfgang Piddlehopper Von Spitzen, who didn't use a whistle. Instead, he would yodel.

Somewhere, a puce and pea-green band was playing, featuring nothing but *spitzentootles*. Adolph, Piffle's dog, was singing *Mein Pretzelsteiner Gal*.

Refreshments were served at the after-the-game social. Norma Jean Bissell, resplendent in a gown of fuzzy wool, belted by a garden hose, was also wearing a sign that read DANGER . . . HIGH VOLTAGE. Norma Jean was serving molasses kisses to everyone else.

To me, the emotional kind.

When she wasn't hanging colored streamers, Miss Boland was juggling three red sink plungers, all of which sparkled in the dark. Then she stopped her juggle act long enough to prepare a hot *Braunschweiger* stew . . . over a Sterno stove.

Soup and I ate a bowl of Soppies.

Everyone seemed, somehow, to be naturally connected with one particular kind of food.

Janice was *bratwurst*.

But then Soup and I had to admit that even Janice deserved a snack. So, for a happy ending, we served her something that we knew she'd eat.

It was potato chips and dip.

Sheep dip.

Robert Newton Peck is the author of forty-seven books. *Soup's Hoop* is the eleventh adventure about Soup and Rob, who also star in Peck's ABC-TV Specials. Robert Newton Peck won the 1982 Mark Twain Award and enjoys visiting schools, colleges, educational conventions, and writers conferences to lecture on both fiction and poetry, and to play ragtime piano.

Robert Newton Peck
500 Sweetwater Club Circle
Longwood, FL 32779

Robert Newton Peck and Great Island Karl
(photo credit: Dorrie Peck)